THE UNSEEMLY PROTECTORS

THE UNLIKELY DEFENDERS BOOK 4

LILY SKYY

First Edition: December 2023

ISBN 978-1-960207-52-4 (ebook)
ISBN 978-1-960207-53-1 (paperback)

Published by Books to Hook Publishing, LLC.
www.BooksToHook.com

CONTENTS

PROLOGUE

Albus Bridge had been a fine, wise, talented, magical being. He helped a group of five teenage kids learn the meaning of the gifts they happened across, and he helped them on their journey of what had become their responsibility to do—save and protect the earth from the great Yash's destruction.

The five teenage kids had relied on Albus's help. And now that he was done, dead because of them, Trace Henderson had not a clue how they were going to go on without him.

Close the portal to all evil beings only, he thought to himself as he shook his head while simultaneously wiping the sweat off if it. *We're so stupid. We should have just done what Albus wanted in the first place. He would still be here if we had.*

Trace was full of rage inside. But, as the quintets worked quietly beside each other to bury Albus, he had to contain it. All Albus had wanted was for them to work together. For them to learn how to be a team. It was the least he could do for the old man now, despite the feelings he was harboring toward the others, mainly his own girlfriend, Amberly McHenry.

Trace being angry inside was not a new feeling for him. It had always been there. In fact, he was almost certain it was a trait he had inherited from his father. Trace let that rage out often, finding uses for it at St. Bernard High School, where it allowed him to easily climb his way to the top. Kaos helped, too, landing him "gigs," as Trace liked to call them, so that Trace could physically fight people and make money doing it, too.

But what people didn't know about Trace was that he hated this trait of his. He hated that he had any similarity to his father at all. It was bad enough that he also had his father's same beefy, muscular build, but he got his straight, sharp nose and his stupid blonde hair from him, too. His mother, Vivian, never stopped pointing it out to him.

Trace didn't want to be like his father. But still, he knew that if anyone had met his father and then met Trace, they would say Trace was Calvin's mini-me.

Trace supposed he had found one good way to release all of his anger—with his sword, the Pentfire. He used it to fight and slay Yash's minions. It felt good. He was putting his anger to good use. He was ridding the world of evil. It was the only time he felt that his anger helped him more than it hindered him.

Still, those flames on his sword had been weak lately. And Trace knew very well the reason why.

As the group finished the burial, Trace slowly got to his feet with the others, remembering the words Albus had told him the day he received the Pentfire.

To control the fire outside, you must first learn to master the raging flame inside of you.

1

The question hung silently in the air between Trace Henderson, Kire Hunter, Amberly McHenry, Charlie Rose, and Kaos Miles after they finished the burial for Albus.

What do we do now?

It was Kaos, who liked to think of himself as the leader of the group, who cleared his throat, the first of the five of them to make any noise in quite some time. "I guess... it's time to go back to Earth."

Currently, they were in the Albus realm, a place they all arrived via a magical portal hidden in a cave in their realm, a place full of other Albuses and other magical creatures. The land around them resembled a fairytale. Or, it used to, back before the war between them and Yash's minions had begun. Now, the destruction of the Albus realm was everywhere. Smoke in the sky. Buildings blasted apart. Towns deserted.

And lots of death.

Yash, a great, powerful entity, had made it his goal to destroy the earth simply because he could and simply because he thought humans to be weak and foolish with their lack of magical abilities and their obsession over their own emotions. And even after the quintets, who stumbled upon their gifts inside of the cave in The White Forest, destroyed the portal that would allow Yash to get to Earth, Yash had found another way. There was another portal that connected the Albus realm to the Earth realm. Yash had easy access to the Albus realm. So he sent his minions down to clear a path for him to get to the portal. However, once again, the quintets worked to fight off his minions, who took on their forms of magical beasts in this realm and often faced multiple of them at a time. And even though Albus had told them all to destroy the portal completely so no travel between the realms could happen ever again, the quintets had put it upon themselves to find another solution—a way to seal it off to *only* evil beings—that way, Albuses could still travel to Earth freely. They knew it was dangerous, but they didn't learn until the very end that a sacrifice was required. Before Rose or Amberly could try and make themselves the sacrifice, Albus ended his own life instead.

It hadn't been what Albus wanted. And Trace would never forget the look on the old man's face right before he plunged the knife into himself, completing the seal.

The minions they had been in the middle of fighting—a griffin, troll, and evil fairy—all disappeared as soon as they learned the portal had been sealed to all evil beings, including Yash. And Trace knew it was because they had gone back to Yash's "ship" to tell him the news.

And now, while Trace was angry at himself for what they caused Albus to have to do, he was also mad at his girlfriend. Had Amberly not thought of him at *all* before she tried to sacrifice herself? Did she not care about him? About leaving him behind?

Of course she doesn't care about you, Trace thought to himself as he avoided any eye contact with her. She had been distant from him for *weeks* now. She had been acting like she wanted nothing to do with him. And all the times they were together, they had gotten into a fight or argument. It wasn't like them. They used to be so good together. The rulers of their high school. Now what were they?

"When we do go back," Kire said, the next to speak, "what is going to be waiting for us?" Kire thought he was as much a leader as Kaos. He was incredibly smart, and he had recently proven to be good at soccer, too, which instantly made him climb the poultry pole at school. The only thing that dragged him down a bit wasn't a thing but a *who*. Charlie, who preferred to be called *Rose*, was a plant-loving nerd, and even though Trace had grown to like her, Amberly was always complaining about how she lowered not just Kire's coolness meter but all of theirs by a lot.

"You mean—you think Rezin is going to be there, ready to fight?" Amberly asked. Trace didn't look at her to see her expression. He didn't want to accidentally meet her gaze. He was too upset and hurt by her.

"Yeah," Kire said.

"Can you talk to Halo?" Rose asked in a squeaky, small voice. She was holding Kire's hand tightly, as if she never planned on letting it go, and Trace understood why. Kire had nearly died during their last battle, and it had been the contents of a vial in a bag Albus left behind that saved him. Rose and Kire had been having little love-spats of their own, but upon realizing they could have lost each other, they now seemed closer than ever.

Realizing Trace almost lost Amberly did not make him want to go and hold *her* hand, though. Kire hadn't meant to nearly die.

Amberly had.

Kire kneeled down, having to let go of Rose's hand to do so, and opened the old leather-bound book called *Halo* that he had been gifted inside of The White Forest's cave. It wrote itself, but in a language only Kire could decipher. So no one else in the group bothered to even try reading over his shoulder as ink appeared on a blank page.

Kire looked grim when he lifted his eyes to meet theirs.

"What?" Trace asked, his stomach dipping. He knew it wasn't good news.

"She's just saying to be prepared."

Kaos clapped his hands together loudly before straightening his crown. "All right, then. Back to the portal. Come on."

He started walking, and reluctantly, the others followed.

"Be prepared," Kaos called over his shoulder, "like Halo said. Get ready for a fight. And try and focus harder on the fact that the five of us are a team, got it? Or else we don't stand a chance."

Trace tried to change his mindset. Their lives depended on it. Rezin was Yash's right-hand man and, therefore, the hardest creature to defeat. For one, he could mess with them all in their dreams. And two, he could make himself invisible, so the gang never knew how to fight back whenever he attacked.

I have a feeling this isn't going to go well, Trace thought to himself. The group had fought terribly in their last battle. And now they were all sad over Albus. And a lot of them still had issues that were unresolved with one another.

They reached the glowing blue portal. It sat in a clearing in the middle of a tall cornfield, tucked away out of sight. On the other side of it, in the Earth realm, they would arrive at the bottom of a lake inside of a cave. Amberly, using her telekinesis gifted to her by her gauntlet, Gamora, had drained the lake and hidden its passage in the cave so no one else could happen upon it.

The portal, with its magnificent arches and winding vines that covered them, didn't look any different after Albus's sacrifice. But seeing as the beasts they had been in the middle of fighting disappeared, Trace knew that it had to have worked. Only those with good intentions would be allowed to travel back and forth now.

"Are we ready?" Kaos asked the others.

"Ready," they all answered, regardless of whether they meant it or not.

Kaos nodded, and he stepped through the portal first. Kire went next, then Rose. Amberly paused, and Trace wondered if maybe she was about to say something to him. But instead, she sighed and went through the portal next.

Trace steeled himself and entered last. His feet lifted off the ground. His stomach rolled. His body felt drenched. But before there was even time to process it, he landed on hard ground with a thud.

They were back on Earth. And because of the way time worked in the Albus realm, it had only been mere minutes since they left it.

They were inside the cave. Trace gripped the smooth, honey-colored wooden handle of his sword tightly. He would draw it out the second he saw Rezin—or felt his presence.

However, the cave was quiet around them.

"I don't think he's here," Amberly said.

"Yeah," Kire, her brother, agreed. "I don't sense him."

"Be on your guard anyway," Kaos said before turning to address Trace, his best friend. "We could use the light from your sword to guide the way."

"Oh, right." They could only see slightly now because of the glow from the portal, but the further they walked away from it, the darker it was going to get.

Trace took the Pentfire from its scabbard. The two-and-a-half-foot-long blade glided out smoothly, and as soon as it was freed, it erupted with fire that snaked its way up Trace's arm, but he couldn't feel it. The blade was beautifully made, shaped like a meandering river with a deadly tip. A golden dragon sat on the rain guard, one of its wings extended up to the fuller.

The fire could have been stronger, but since the Defenders weren't getting along well, their fighting skills and magical abilities were suffering. Albus told them they were strongest when they were united.

They had work to do to make that happen again.

The entire walk out of the cave, no one said anything. It was as if they were afraid they'd alert Rezin of their presence if they did. That, or they simply just had nothing to say to each other.

An uneasy sensation overtook Trace when they approached the cave's mouth. And by the way everyone slowed in their step behind him, he knew they felt it, too.

Still, they exited. And when they did, a figure stood, waiting.

At first, Trace had no idea what, or *who*, he was looking at. Then he realized it was a person. But it was late at night—what was a person—especially one in a nice tux—doing out in The White Forest at this time? And why were they wearing sunglasses over their eyes?

"You must be thinking pretty highly of yourselves," the man said. His voice was chilling and deep.

Everyone tensed.

Before them, the man merely chuckled. "You've had your fun, *children*. But now, your time is over. It's *my* turn."

Trace was just beginning to register that this man in the sunglasses was actually Rezin and that they were seeing him for the first time before he felt his body lift in the air and heard the screams from Rose and Amberly.

Trace was thrown back with force. He slammed into a thick tree trunk and lost his grip on his sword, whose flames immediately diminished the second his fingers were no longer touching it.

He cried out but was quick to get back to his feet and back to his sword. He saw Rezin, who had ripped his sunglasses off and was revealing to them sockets of fire where his eyes were supposed to be. He laughed, and as Rose tried to manipulate some vines to wrap around his body and restrain him, he merely glanced down at them, and they shriveled away from him and crumbled to dust.

Seeing this, Rose looked petrified. Trace charged Rezin as he lifted Rose into the air next. He threw her back, and before Trace reached him, Rose manipulated a bunch of leaves to cushion her landing.

"He's going to use his mind to make you hallucinate!" Kaos yelled at Trace, using his crown to get inside Rezin's mind. Then, suddenly, Trace saw nothing but pitch-black emptiness all around him.

What is happening?

Trace feared to take another step. It was as if he had been transported somewhere. Then, out of the darkness, a lion made of fire started barreling toward him, having appeared out of thin air. Trace turned and started running, even though he couldn't see where he was going, and then his body slammed into something hard, and he fell to the ground again, momentarily losing consciousness.

When he came to, he was back in The White Forest, and it was complete chaos. As much as the other Defenders were trying to fight against Rezin, who could disappear out of thin air and reappear wherever and whenever he wanted, they weren't good enough to overpower him. Trace was terrified that this fight was going to end badly.

There was only one thing they could do right now to get out of here alive.

Run.

He got to his feet, his head pounding, and as soon as Rezin was standing in one spot, focused on trying to get through Halo's protective shield around Kire, Trace ran in a wide circle around him with his sword, catching every bit of the forest around him on fire as he went.

With Rezin surrounded by the flames, Trace and the others stared in amazement. Barricaded in like this, Rezin seemed weakened, unable to disappear or teleport. He yelled out in rage.

"Guys, come on!" Trace bellowed, motioning for them to run with him. The other four didn't hesitate as the fire rapidly spread, making them all begin to choke on the smoke.

They had escaped Rezin yet again. But they couldn't run forever.

2

Trace was sulking.

He was in his backyard, slowly kicking his soccer ball around the dead, half-frozen grass that was never tended to. He had school today, but he opted to skip it. The only person he told he wasn't going other than his mother was Kaos since Kaos always came to pick him up in the mornings. Kaos had told him he was faking sick, too. Trace wasn't the only one who lacked the motivation to go back to school after what had happened to them yesterday.

Albus had died.

Trace looked up at the sky, unable to keep his eyes away for too long at a time. It looked like the end of the world in their town of Montgomery. The fire in The White Forest was still ablaze, and it had grown and spread rapidly. There was a thick black cloud in the distance, and everything around him was coated in a gray haze. The sky was orange, reflecting the flames. Ash was falling and landing on Trace like snowflakes.

He coughed, knowing he should go inside. But he didn't want to face his mom. He didn't feel like talking. This fire was his fault. Albus had always been around to clean up their messes after another attack from one of Yash's minions, like Heno or Jago, but he was gone now, and it allowed the fire to spread like a cancer.

Trace regretted what he did to distract Rezin so they could all make their escape. But what choice had he had? Rezin was going to destroy them otherwise. They weren't powerful enough to fight back. Not yet. It reminded Trace of a video game. Rezin was a boss, and Trace's character hadn't reached a high enough level in order to be able to defeat him, so any attempt at trying to do so before then was futile. Pointless.

He knew that in order for them to gain the strength they had once upon a time—when they had first fought some of Yash's minions in the Albus realm after becoming more united than they had ever been, it had been almost too easy to destroy them—they had to get back to that union. They had to get over all of their issues with each other. And even once they did that, it would probably be wise for them to actually *plan* something. A way to defeat Rezin once and for all. They had just gone into it last night blindly, and that wasn't going to work, even if they had been stronger as a unit.

But Trace didn't have the first clue how to go about fixing things with Amberly. He was still a wreck over what she had tried to do yesterday. He felt abandoned by her. Just as he had been abandoned by his father long ago. He knew Amberly didn't think her sacrifice was selfish, but that was *all* he thought about it. *Not everyone gets to take the easy way out,* he thought. *Why should she?*

When the smoke lingering in the air became a little bit too much for him, and he was coughing more and more, he finally retreated back into his small, humble home. He lived in a simple one-story in a slightly shady neighborhood. Trace never had people over, really, because of how ashamed he was of the life home life he had. People saw the popular and mighty Trace, the apex predator, at school and probably did not think at all that he was as poor as he was. But when his father left him and his mother when Trace was a young boy, his mother fell into some bad habits and had a hard time ever keeping a job. In fact, even right now in their life, it seemed as if Trace's mother relied on him to make most of their income, even though Trace had so much other stuff to focus on, like … saving the world. And much less, school.

"Hi, honey. Did the fresh air do you any good?" Vivian asked when Trace stepped into the kitchen from outside. He could see, all the way from where he stood by the door that was inside the kitchen, into the living room. He could practically see the whole house from any spot he was standing; that's how small it was.

His mother was lounging on their old sofa with a blanket that probably hadn't been washed in weeks draped over her. She coughed and smiled at him, her eyes droopy. The TV was on in the background, but it was muted because she wanted to talk to him.

Trace didn't feel like talking, but he didn't want to upset her either. He loved his mother. She was perhaps the most important person on this planet to him.

"Mom, can you not see what it looks like outside from there?" Trace had opened the blinds this morning even though his mother preferred to keep them closed. He, himself, could still see how fiery the sky was, and he was much further from the window than she was.

She turned and looked out the window as if she was just then realizing the blinds were open.

"Goodness! That's just horrible," she said. "What were you even doing out there?"

Trace rolled his eyes and laughed, walking over to join her in the living room. He took a seat in the old leather recliner. The surface of it was cracking and flaking off in pieces more and more every time he sat down. Their whole house was like this, filled with old furniture that hadn't been replaced since he was a baby.

"I know, Mom," he said. "That's why I came back in."

"Are you still feeling sick?"

"It's not so bad," he said, feeling horrible for lying to his mother. he had already done so much of that when it came to The Unlikely Defenders. His mom couldn't know what he was up to. But before he had started to need to lie about that, he had hardly ever lied to his mom about anything.

"That's good. I don't want you to fall behind," she said.

His guilty conscience just grew guiltier. She also was not aware that he wasn't doing so hot in school. But how was he supposed to focus on some stupid essays and math worksheets when he had such a huge responsibility?

"Don't worry about me," he told her, reaching out to pat her foot that was sticking out of the blanket. "Just worry about you."

She swatted a hand dismissively. "Nothing to worry about with me," she replied. But it wasn't true at all. His mother was sick. She had a liver disease. It was why Trace was always trying to make money. On top of paying for their bills, and with a little assistance they got from the government, they also didn't have health insurance, so they had to pay for his mother's medication for her liver disease out of pocket.

And it was expensive.

Yes, there were so many other things Trace could be spending the money on, like getting himself some counseling for all of his anger, saving up to be able to go to college someday or buying himself a car, but his mother was sick, and her needs came first.

"Whatever you say," Trace said, smiling. His mother was one of the only people who got to see him smiling. His friends and Amberly were the only other ones.

On the TV in front of them, a news broadcast came on, and seeing that it was about the fire in The White Forest, his mother un-muted the TV with the remote. Trace tried not to listen, but it was impossible to miss the words "Massive destruction" and "Devastating to our ecosystem."

So he stood up. "You know what, I think I need to go back to bed," he told his mother.

"Sounds good," she said with a yawn. "I'll probably take a nap here, too."

Trace kissed the top of her head and then retreated back to his small bedroom. Inside of it, he barely had room for a twin bed, a dresser, and a clothing hamper in the corner. He flopped down on his always unmade bed and pulled his phone out of his pocket. He had missed text messages from the quintets' group chat. But he didn't feel like opening the thread to see what they were saying.

He hadn't lied to his mom *completely* about why he didn't want to go to school today. He still felt sore from all of the fighting he had done yesterday. Even though since he had become an unlikely defender, he had gained immortality and quick healing abilities, it wasn't as if he no longer felt any pain.

Eventually, with thoughts about Amberly and how he was reluctant to have to face her again tomorrow, he fell asleep for the majority of the day.

TRACE'S head felt a little bit better, more screwed on when he woke up from his long nap. The sun had set outside, but still, the street lights in front of his house illuminated the surroundings, and Trace could still see the orange hue in the air. The White Forest fire was still blazing, and he wished there was something he could do to tame it.

He left his phone on the table beside his bed. He wasn't ready to deal with his friends yet, but he knew that he wanted to try to become better as a team. He knew he had to push things aside. They had a big fight coming with Rezin, and it was crucial to their survival that they beat him once and for all.

Despite the air and how he had started choking on it when he had been outside earlier, Trace managed to sneak into his backyard again, unseen by his mother, who seemed like she hadn't moved on the couch since Trace saw her earlier that day. His mom never came into the backyard, so she never spotted him when he was working with the Pentfire, watching YouTube videos on his dusty laptop given to him by Kaos a couple years ago as he practiced his swords-manship.

His sword could also blast fire from it at directed targets, and Kire often practiced with old cardboard boxes. He placed them all around his backyard and used them as his targets, aiming the flaming balls of fire at them, which were similar to the ones Rezin could shoot out of his eyeballs.

Trace practiced for so long that he lost track of time and again, only went back inside when the air became too unbearable. He felt good about his swordsmanship. He knew he had skill. He had been practicing for quite some time now, pretty much ever since he was first gifted the sword.

But he knew that his skills alone wouldn't be what made him a good fighter when it came down to a battle with Rezin. He needed all five of the quintets to be skillful, and they all needed to be able to use their powers together.

3

After Trace had hidden his sword back safely in his bedroom, he wandered into the kitchen and whipped himself up a freezer meal. He was starving from all the training, and he had slept so much that day that he hadn't had a single bite to eat.

The ruckus of him moving around in the kitchen stirred his mom over on the couch.

"Throw one in for me, too, will you?" Vivian asked as she sat up and stretched. Even in the darkness of the living room, Trace could see how pale she looked.

"Are you sure?" Trace asked. "It's late. Maybe you should just go to bed and wait for breakfast? Or did you not have dinner?"

"I lost track of time, to be honest," she replied.

He squinted at her. She suddenly looked wide awake. And her eyes were searching the room. She was thinking of a plan, and Trace wasn't sure it was one he wanted to know about.

"Okay," he said flatly, heating her up a microwave meal as well. It wasn't that he cared that she wanted to eat when it was after midnight; it was more that he would prefer she just go to bed so that he knew exactly what it was she was doing when he went to bed as well.

"Thanks, handsome," she told him.

"Welcome."

She got herself up from the sofa, albeit weakly, and joined him in the kitchen. When both meals were heated, they sat together at the counter and ate.

"You're gonna go to bed after this?" Trace asked her.

"Are you?" she deadpanned.

Her ice-blue eyes, the same as his, peered into his mischievously. Questioningly.

"Yep—I sure am. Gotta get enough rest for school tomorrow."

"Good. I'm almost due for a refill, too, by the way."

"Already?" Trace was quickly losing his appetite. Did he have enough to buy her a refill of medication yet? He'd have to go check his stash, but he was nearly certain he didn't. He needed to come up with some more cash stat.

"I know the days go by quickly," she told him. "I really do appreciate how helpful you are, honey."

"It's no big deal," Trace said. "You know how I'd do anything for you."

She leaned over and kissed him on the cheek. He groaned and wiped the slobber off him. "Enough of the cheesiness."

She pursed her lips. "You got it, boss."

After dinner, Trace said goodnight to his mom, who claimed that she was going to stay up and watch TV in the living room until she fell asleep. Then he hopped in the shower and crawled back into bed even though he had spent the majority of the day in it.

When he checked his phone again, he had no new messages. No one else has reached out to him since the messages in the group chat. Still ignoring them and not opening the thread, Trace wondered what Amberly was up to at that moment. Yes, it was late, but maybe she was still awake. When she had tried to sacrifice herself, she had told Rose that her life wasn't meaningful. He wondered if she still felt this way. And he had an urge to text her or call her. To check if she was still alive.

He was worried about his girlfriend. She just lost her mother, and it couldn't be easy to deal with it. Trace couldn't even imagine what it would be like if he lost Vivian. And like Trace, it wasn't as if Amberly had another parent she could lean on. She was stuck with her new aunt, and Trace didn't even know if Amberly liked her or not. There was so much that he didn't know about her anymore. They had never been so distant from each other before.

Instead of texting his girlfriend, Trace eventually fell back asleep.

It wasn't long before he started to dream. He was home, in this house that he had always lived in. And he was still the same teenager that he was now. But yet, things were different at his house. His dad, Calvin, lived with them again. And he looked just as he had when he left, even though his mother looked much older. Like she did now.

Trace was happy. His mom looked happy. His dad was smiling, too. They were all sitting around the usually unused table in the dining area—they preferred to eat their meals at the counter— sharing a meal. Trace looked down at his plate and saw the eggs and bacon, signaling that it was breakfast time.

And while Trace was happy that all three of them were together, he felt a little on edge, too. The smile on his face felt a little forced, only because he was desperate to show his father that he was glad he was there.

Calvin Henderson looked like a successful businessman. He was wearing a well-tailored suit, and his blond hair, the same exact shade as Trace's, was gelled back stylishly. He had an expensive watch on his wrist and shiny gold cufflinks.

Calvin had the type of face that, when he smiled, lit up a room and made women weak at the knees. But it was the sort of face that, when angry, could twist and become the most hideous thing you've ever seen. Trace was desperate to make sure he didn't see that side of his dad during their meal.

"So, Trace," his father started, wiping his mouth on a napkin. "I heard a rumor at work."

"What kind of a rumor?" Trace asked. His dad's tone was still casual and light, which had to be a good sign, right?

"I heard from some colleagues that the fire in The White Forest was started by some teenager. You wouldn't happen to know anything about that, would you?"

That was when his look changed. His father's eyes narrowed in on him. His eyebrows lowered. The smile slipped away.

How could he have any idea what Trace had done?

"I—I don't know," Trace tried. He sat frozen in his seat, the butter knife in one hand and the fork in the other.

"You don't... *know*?"

"I promise," Trace tried. But even as he told the lie, he knew his father wouldn't believe him. He should've just gone with the truth instead. But how could he even begin to explain to him why the fire started?

Calvin turned to Vivian. "What were you thinking letting him leave the house, anyway?" he asked her, his tone icy.

"You're right," she said, looking down at her plate, too fearful to make eye contact with him. "I should have told him he needed to stay home."

"No, Mom, it's not your fault," Trace said. "I snuck out." He didn't want his mom covering for him. She had done so before, and it hadn't led to anything good.

Calvin only seemed to grow angrier. He stood up quickly, his chair screeching along the old wooden flooring. "So which is it then?" he snapped to Vivian. "Are you lying to me, or is it my *son* lying to me?"

Both Trace and his mother were silent.

That was when his dad started screaming.

And that was when Trace and his mother were turned into his punching bags.

With the beatings, Trace squeezed his eyes shut and just waited for it to be over. It wasn't anything new. It had happened before. Many, many times. He just kept telling himself, *It will be over soon.*

But when he opened his eyes to peek at his father, he no longer saw Calvin. Instead, a purple creature was wailing on him. It had six arms. And all the head had on it was a mouth. Not even eyes. It made sickening screeching noises. The whole thing looked like it had been some sort of experiment gone wrong and a science lab.

But the punches hurt. Trace could physically feel each and every one of them.

"Stop!" Trace yelled.

"Not until you're dead."

It was no longer the voice of his father. Now, it was Rezin talking to him. Rezin had started manipulating his dream.

Thinking quickly, knowing now that this was a dream, that his dad wasn't really back, he knew he could manipulate his dream as well. He willed his Pentfire to appear. It manifested out of thin air right into his open hand, and he closed his fist around the handle and immediately shot a fireball at Rezin. Finally, the alien creature was thrown backward, and the pain was beginning to slowly subside.

"We won't let you win, Rezin!" Trace shouted. And then, upon wanting to make sure he had the last word, he woke himself from the dream, where the blows from his dad and Rezin were still causing him physical pain in real life. But that was just a nasty trick of Rezin's—he could make what happened in your dreams real.

And to Trace, it had felt so, so real.

"Man," Trace said as he threw the blankets off him and stood up, his entire body drenched in sweat. "We have *got* to get rid of him."

After he was able to calm his breathing, he went into the

kitchen to grab an ice pack out of the freezer. He had a shiner right there on his face, and he had no way to explain it to his mother.

He noticed, only able to use one eye because the other one was covered with a frozen bag of peas, that Vivian had never gotten up to go to bed last night. And around her, the evidence was plain—Vivian had gone on another one of her bingers last night. Trace didn't even know where she had been hiding her stash this time.

To cope with all of the trauma she had endured in her life, and because her heart was so badly broken when their father walked out on them, Vivian developed a bad drinking problem. It was why she developed the liver disease in the first place. And yet, even though she was sick, she couldn't stop her drinking habits. Yes, she had told Trace over and over that she wanted to stop drinking, but it never actually happened.

Trace, who was a bit of a clean freak, immediately got started cleaning up after his mom, picking up empty bottle after empty bottle and all of the trash from when she had apparently decided to have a snack feast sometime in the middle of the night.

All the while, Vivian slept soundly on the sofa, nothing loud enough to stir her. Trace knew she would have a killer headache when she woke up—which wouldn't be until probably after he got back from school—but just in case, he set a fresh glass of water and some pain reliever pills next to her orange prescription bottle that contained her lessening supply of medication for her disease. She would need all of those when she woke up.

The blanket had halfway fallen off his mother, so with a sigh, sick of having to do this with her, sick of seeing her act like this, he tucked her back in and kissed the top of her head. He was past the point of being angry at her. Besides, he never wanted to have a temper with her, not after he had to watch what she went through with his father way back when. When it came to Vivian, Trace was just sad. He wished he could help her. But he knew she was sick in more ways than one. Alcoholism was a disease in itself. One that took a lot of effort to fix. One that there was not one simple magical cure for.

Trace was beginning to feel overwhelmed by all of his stress. His mother couldn't even begin to understand everything else he was dealing with on top of this. So it wasn't exactly her fault he was a ball of emotion ready to explode. If he didn't do something soon about everything going on in his life, Trace worried he was going to explode into such a fit of rage that he never calmed down from it.

After cleaning up, as he hurried to get ready with the little time he had left before Kaos would be here to pick him up for school, Trace told himself that it was time for him to take action.

4

Not wanting to chance that Kaos would try to come into Trace's house and risk him seeing Vivian like that, Trace was already waiting for Kaos's arrival in his shiny red car out on the curb outside of his house. He gave his best friend a nod when he pulled up and hopped into the passenger seat.

"I was wondering if you died," Kaos said. As always, he was wearing all black like he had some funeral to attend. Kaos was tall but had a slimmer build than Trace. A lot of times, Trace felt as if he was some sort of caged-in animal and that Kaos was his ringmaster. Kaos made all of their plans and controlled every decision. He had a say over everything, and Trace let him. Kaos had always been a good friend to Trace, and he was helpful when it came to him needing money for the drugs for his mother, so he couldn't risk their friendship falling apart. Especially now with everything else going on in his life.

"I told you I wasn't going to school yesterday," Trace reminded him.

"Yeah, but you never replied to the group chat."

"I didn't even open it. I was just... busy. What were you guys saying?"

"Just that we all need to work on our training and reconvene as soon as possible."

"You weren't talking about the fire that I started at all?" Trace raised an eyebrow.

Kaos shrugged. "Fine. We mentioned that, too. I can't believe it's still so bad."

"We forgot that we have to pick up after ourselves now."

They drove in silence for a bit. Trace knew they were on their way to pick up Amberly next. But he didn't know how he felt about it. "I'm not sure I'm ready to face Amberly," he finally admitted.

"What are you talking about?"

"I..." He didn't even know where to begin. He turned in his seat so his entire body was facing Kaos. "Dude. I've been doing everything you've told me to to get things back on track with Amberly. To get her to like me again. To be the old us. But honestly, I feel like your advice has sort of made everything worse. Giving her space has only made her question if I even like her at *all*. I think it might've even made her think that I wouldn't care if she died. Or else she wouldn't have... you know."

"I don't think it's really about you," Kaos told him. "She's going through a lot right now, ya know?"

"Obviously. I *am* her boyfriend."

They couldn't further the discussion because they had just pulled up to Amberly's new house, where her aunt lived.

Amberly walked out the door in sunglasses, looking beautiful as always. Her long blonde hair was pulled into a tight, sleek ponytail, showing off her sharp, striking facial features. She was wearing a leather skirt, tights, and high-heeled furry boots. When she climbed into the backseat, all she gave was a simple, "Hey," and Trace didn't even know if it was directed at him or Kaos.

"Sleep good?" Kaos asked her, being the one to keep the conversation flowing as he resumed driving.

"Sort of. I'm just glad it wasn't another night tormented by Rezin in my sleep."

Trace had been about to mention how Rezin had decided to torment *his* dream instead, but he decided against it. Still, he wasn't sure who Amberly was talking to, and he was worried that if he opened his mouth, she would just tell him to shut up.

"Aren't you glad you even got to sleep at all?" Kaos asked her. Trace snuck a glance at her to find her sneering at Kaos.

"What is *that* supposed to mean?" she asked in her snooty voice.

"If you had sacrificed yourself, you wouldn't get to sleep ever again."

"Okay?" She rolled her eyes. "I would be dead... so I wouldn't even know whether or not I was getting any sleep."

"I'm just saying," Kaos replied.

Trace could tell that he wasn't the only one affected by the fact that Amberly had tried to sacrifice herself. Kaos and Amberly were friends, too. She had almost left him, too.

"Where are we going?" Amberly asked, abruptly changing the subject, her tone still full of attitude.

"Where do you think?" Kaos asked back. "We're going to get Kire and then Rose."

Amberly groaned aloud.

"You know the rules," Kaos said. "No more of that, Amberly."

"I mean, I'm *fine* with us getting *Kire*," Amberly explained.

During their last battle, Trace had caught a glimpse of how it seemed Kire and Amberly may have resolved the conflict with each other. Were they now going to act like a normal couple of siblings? Or were they going to quickly go back to being each other's enemies?

"You have to be cool with Rose, too," Kaos said.

She crossed her arms. "Fine."

She pouted the rest of the way to picking up Kire.

Kire slid into the middle seat. "What's up with her?" he asked the guys, motioning to Amberly, who was facing out the window with her sunglasses still on.

"Just the typical Amberly," Kaos said. Beside him, Trace was still being silent.

Charlie Rose was next on the carpool list. She walked out of her house wearing a floral long-sleeve shirt and old faded jeans. She had flowers in her hair, like she usually did.

"Plant freak," Amberly muttered. Beside her, Kire swatted at her. Like a brother would.

As Rose entered the backseat, she also had a pouty look on her face.

"What's wrong?" Kire asked immediately.

She closed the door and buckled herself in. "Don't get me wrong, I get why you did what you did yesterday to get us out of there, Trace, and I am super grateful, but... That poor forest!"

"Yeah, I wasn't thinking about the aftermath when I did it," Trace said.

"I know that there are firefighters on it and all that," Kaos said, "but do you think we should, like... skip school and try to help them contain it? Discreetly use our powers or something?"

"I was wondering that, too," Amberly said, suddenly back to engaging in conversation. "But I feel that it's just too risky. We could get caught. And then how would we explain ourselves?"

"Maybe they would think we were just trying to do a good deed?" Kire tried.

"With our crown, gauntlet, sword, weird necklace, and super old book?" Amberly countered.

"She's right," Trace said, agreeing with his girlfriend, even though his tone was dark. "It's too risky. We just gotta hope that the firefighters can get a handle on it soon."

5

For Trace, the rest of the ride to school was borderline unbearable. Amberly was his girlfriend, and they were acting as if they hardly even knew each other. It was as if, right before his very eyes, Amberly was slipping away from him. And they were both so dang stubborn; neither one of them felt that they were the one in the wrong. But how could Amberly not understand how upset and hurt he was by what she had tried to do back in the Albus realm?

Trace just desperately wanted to know what Amberly had been thinking when she nearly ended her own life. And he also desperately wanted to know what she was thinking now.

Why do girls have to be so dang confusing? he thought to himself as the gang pulled into the school parking lot in Kaos's car. Trace noticed the way, as usual, that everybody on campus seemed to turn their heads and look at Kaos's red beauty. The quintets had a pretty high "social status," and that even seemed to include Rose nowadays, too, since she had been hanging out with them. Trace had noticed recently the way that more people seemed to be interested in talking to Rose. How fewer people seemed to be teasing her all the time. In fact, he was pretty sure he saw one of his peers starting to put flowers in her own hair, and he suspected that Rose was the one who had started the trend. He wondered if more people were going to start following in her footsteps as well.

They all get out of the car, and Kaos and Amberly walk together ahead of the other three.

"Are you guys just not going to talk for... forever?" Kire asked Trace, referring to him and Amberly. "This must be super awkward for you."

"Yeah." Trace balled his fists. "It is." Then, just like that, his mind was made up.

He marched ahead of Kire and Rose and reached Kaos and Amberly. He took Amberly's hand and turned her around to him. "Hey," he said to her. His voice was dark. "Can we please talk?"

They were still in the parking lot. They hadn't quite made it to the front of the school, where most of their classmates hung out before the first bell rang.

"Um..." Amberly ripped her hand away from Trace. Her perfectly arched eyebrows furrowed closely together, and she stared at him as if he had no right to be holding her hand. As if she had no idea who he was and he was just some creep. Not her boyfriend.

"Come on," Trace tried. "I really think we need to have a serious talk." He felt uncomfortable with the rest of the gang around to hear what he was saying to Amberly. And he felt even *more* uncomfortable when Amberly stuck her nose in the air and sneered at him.

"I can't do this with you right now." And then she grabbed Kaos's elbow and dragged him away from Trace with her, their heads bent together.

That's messed up, Trace thought to himself. Kaos was *his* friend first. He only became Amberly's friend as well after the two of them got into a relationship. And now Amberly thought she could just steal him from Trace?

"Yikes," Rose whispered, catching up with a frozen, angered Trace. "That did not go well."

Trace, annoyed at the comment, simply shook his head and then left Kire and Rose to be the happy couple they were. Inside the school, as he stormed to his locker, he was fuming. It was like something had snapped. Like Amberly had stepped on the twig inside of him, cracking it, splintering it into two pieces, and he couldn't stand it.

I'm not doing this anymore, he told himself when he grabbed the books he needed and slammed his locker door shut so loudly that heads turned to stare at him. He was certain everyone could tell he was in a foul mood today.

Good.

Hopefully, everyone knew to stay out of his way then.

WHEN LUNCH ROLLED AROUND, Trace was a very determined, capable, and angry teenage boy. He stormed into the cafeteria through the double doors. He marched right up to where Amberly was sitting at their usual lunch table next to Kaos.

Trace had taken his time arriving at the cafeteria because he needed to really think over what it was he was going to say to Amberly. How he was going to approach this. But, the second his eyes laid on her, all of his carefully composed ideas flew out the window. All he felt was rage.

"Amberly, let's go," he demanded.

"Excuse me?"

"In the hall." He knew he sounded scary. But he also knew that Amberly was never afraid of him.

"Uh, hello? I'm eating," she snapped.

"No, you're not. You hardly ever eat lunch here." She didn't even have a lunch tray in front of her. Trace knew we had her there.

She stared at him for a long while, her jaw jutting and her nostrils flaring, before finally, she stood up. "Fine."

Trace led the way, shooting Kaos a stolid expression before he turned around because he couldn't help but feel a stab of anger toward him, too—why was he letting Amberly treat him this way?

They went out into the hall, where they could have some privacy for this conversation.

"What is your problem?" Amberly asked from behind, being the first to speak. When Trace finally turned around to stare at her, her arms were crossed, and she had a hip jutting out. She looked impatient, like she didn't want his conversation to take long.

He didn't care how long it took. He needed to get through to her.

"What is *my* problem?" He shook his head. "Amberly, why are you being like this?"

"Being like what?"

"Like... like... you don't care about m—anything." Trace had been about to say "me," but he didn't want to sound like a whiny baby. "Like you don't want to talk to me or be around me. I need to understand exactly what the heck it is I did to you."

"I'm surprised you even want to talk to me at all," she said. Trace could see the pain in her expression. She was trying to cover it up, but for once, she wasn't doing that great of a job.

"What are you talking about?" Trace asked. "I don't understand what's been going on with you lately. Why you've been so mad at me. Why you tried to... do that, back in You-Know-Where." He looked over his shoulder. He didn't want anybody to overhear him talking about going to another realm.

"Oh, *come* on, you have to stop being so upset about that."

"Don't tell me what I have to do, Amberly."

"I was trying to save the human race."

"Yeah. And leave us all behind. Why do you think that would be what any of us wanted?"

He couldn't stop seeing her during that fight in the Albus realm.

The look of resignation on her face. The look that told Trace she had made up her mind. That there was going to be no stopping her. She seemed worried about her brother, who lay dying, sure. But that had been the only emotion on her face whatsoever. She seemed so ready to just... go.

In the hall, Amberly looked away from him.

"I know that you're dealing with a lot," Trace continued. "I know you have a bunch of crap going on with your dad and Kire and your mom passing. I've been trying to keep doing the right thing. To give you the space that you need. I've been trying *so* hard, Amberly, to do everything right so that you don't push me away, too. But despite my efforts, I'm still failing."

"You... You think you've been trying, Trace?"

"It's all I've been doing."

"Are you kidding me?" she jeered. "You haven't seemed like you're trying at all! I hardly ever hear from you. I really needed you, Trace, after my mom died. And you just weren't there. You didn't even try to be."

"I... I didn't know you wanted me around," Trace said. "I thought you needed the space."

"Why would I want space from my boyfriend? Why would I want to be alone after my mom died? What possessed you, at all, to think that? 'Oh, my girlfriend's mom just died, let me ignore her, that will help!'"

"Okay, stop with the sass."

She growled at him. "No, *you* stop, Trace. Stop acting like you are the victim in this. You're the one who messed up. You're the one who became friends with Kire and Rose and suddenly decided that since you had them, it wasn't as important to have me."

"Is that seriously what you think? You are so far from the truth, Amberly. You're... delusional."

"Don't call me that!"

Trace wasn't meaning to name-call. He was just so worked up. Words were flying out of his mouth before he could stop them. He had never been good at picking them carefully. At thinking before he spoke. He got into a lot of trouble because of it.

"Why not?" he pressed on. "It's true! Just like you were *delusional* to think that your life mattered less than anyone else's! When you thought that *Rose's* life was more important than yours!"

"Shut up," she hissed. Trace sensed that was a touchy subject. Amberly would never admit out loud that she thought someone had it better than her. But yet, back in the Albus realm, that's exactly what she had done.

"Don't tell me to shut up," Trace barked. "You know what, Amberly? I have put up with so much from you through this entire relationship!"

"What are you talking about?"

"Of course you don't see it because, like I said, you're *delusional*. You're spoiled. Prissy. Entitled. A bully. Oh, and selfish. So, *so* selfish!"

Even though lunch was ending and people were starting to leave the cafeteria and spill out into the hallway they were in, Trace didn't quiet down. He didn't try to take the conversation with Amberly somewhere else.

And Amberly didn't try to go anywhere else, either.

Her face was reddening. "Oh yeah? And what about you? You want to call *me* a bully? You suck so badly with sorting out your feelings that all you do is go around and beat the crap out of people instead! You're just like this big, dumb brute! You're good at soccer, Trace, and you're good at throwing your fists around, but where is that going to get you after high school, huh?"

"Oh, please. You're so involved in your own life that you don't even know practically anything about mine! After all this time we've been together! You still don't even really know me at all, Amberly!"

"And whose fault is that?!"

"Whose do you think? You can't even be bothered to listen to anyone if they have anything to say that doesn't involve you!"

"I think you need to be looking in the mirror when you say that, Trace! Talk about pot calling the kettle black!"

People were not at all interested in getting to their next class or even in getting stuff out of their lockers to prepare. Instead, all of the students at St. Bernard High seemed much more interested in watching the scene unfold between Trace and Amberly. Not once had the couple had a blowup fight like this in front of people. To everyone, they had always appeared as the perfect ruling duo of the school.

And before all of their eyes, their relationship was crumbling.

"There's no getting through to you!" Trace yelled. He was so tired of this. Tired of the fighting. Tired of feeling like he was constantly doing something wrong. Tired of feeling like she didn't care more about him. He didn't need it. He had enough going on in his life without it.

"Oh yeah, Trace? I'm just *that* horrible of a girlfriend? Gee, I'm sorry that everything I've been through lately isn't enough to excuse me for acting a little on edge! You're right; who cares that my dad wants to pretend like I don't exist? Who cares that I got fired from my job? Who cares that my mom died and my house exploded? Who cares that Albus died? Who cares that my entire life has been flipped upside down? I shouldn't be focused on any of that! I should be focused on catering to you, on being the perfect, doting girlfriend all the time!"

"I tried to help you through all of that!"

"And like most things you do, you sucked at it!"

"Well, if that's the case, you don't have to worry anymore, Amberly."

"What?"

"That's right. If I'm such a sucky boyfriend, then there's no need for you to be wasting your time with me. Tons of guys at the school would kill to be with you. So go shove all your problems at them. Because we are done."

She stuttered and stumbled over her words, clearly unsure of how to react. But Trace could tell she was shocked. Had she really not expected it to end like this? After everything she said to him?

"I—you—well, good!" she managed to get out. "It's about time!"

With a look that made Trace wonder if she was ever going to talk to him again, she turned on her high-heeled, furry boot and disappeared into the crowd of students. Trace turned and punched the nearest locker so hard that he could feel his knuckles instantly split open, and when he pulled it back, the locker door was dented. Around him, people jumped at his reaction.

When he turned to face everyone staring still, his body was a tense, shaking monster. He went up to the first kid he made eye contact with. "What are you staring at, huh?!" he yelled. "I'll punch you next!"

The kid backed away, clearly not wanting to start any drama with him. Trace thought he was smart for doing so.

He scanned the rest of the crowd. "Get out of here! Nobody better mess with me, or I swear, you will regret it for the rest of your life!" He didn't wait to see if his threat worked to make everybody continue on their way. Instead, *he* was the one who shot through the crowd and stormed away, going in the opposite direction of Amberly.

St. Bernard High School's favorite couple was officially, and very publicly, over.

6

Trace couldn't bear to see Amberly during gym class, which was his class right after lunch on Fridays, so he ditched it. He couldn't really bear to see *anyone* right now. Not when he was so angry. So destroyed.

He hadn't wanted to break up with Amberly. He'd never wanted that. He had just been so angry at her. And she had said some really messed up things to him. But they *both* had said messed up things. But still, Trace had been fully convinced even before the fight that Amberly hated him. So, why had she even been wasting her time with him?

This is for the best, he kept trying to tell himself as he paced to the school hallways, avoiding teachers so that he wouldn't get caught skipping gym and then get thrown into detention. Although, he would almost welcome detention right now, and he suspected it was coming soon anyway since he damaged somebody's locker, school property. It wouldn't be the first time.

He could feel his eyes burning with tears over his breakup, and he hated it. Who was he? Trace Henderson didn't cry. He was the one who broke up with her! He should be glad! Relieved!

But instead, he was miserable. His decision to end the relationship had a huge impact on a lot of things, like his friendship with Kaos. Now, Kaos was in the middle of the two of them.

Not to mention, how were they supposed to work well as a team trying to kill Rezin now? They only worked well together when they were united. But Trace didn't want to even have to be in the same room as her. It would just be too hard.

The next class he had after gym on Fridays was his weights class. Thankfully, no one from the quintets was in that class, so Trace decided he didn't need to skip it. Besides, pumping some iron would probably help relieve some of his anger.

While he did his workout, he was so much in his own head that he didn't even see the peculiar way his weight training teacher, Mr. Tillman, was acting. How he was just standing at the front of the room, his arms crossed, sunglasses over his eyes, watching him.

The entire time.

AFTER ECONOMICS, the last class of the day that Trace shared with Kaos, Kire and Rose, his teacher, Miss Wright, informed him on his way out the door that Mr. Tillman wanted to speak with him in the weight training room.

Wondering what it was he did wrong now, he shrugged at Kaos, Kire and Rose, who were staring at him questioningly, and then he walked past them and through the hallway back toward his last class.

As Trace moved through the throng of students, he got a sense that people had already picked their side over their very public breakup. No one wanted to so much as look at him.

Figures, he thought to himself as he ignored the whispered conversations where he could hear his name being mentioned. He had just dumped the girl who just lost her mother. Amberly had also mentioned Albus being dead, and even though no one else knew who he was, Trace was certain they all thought he was another relative of hers. That she was mourning *multiple* deaths. No one knew that Trace was mourning Albus's death, too.

Trace entered the empty weight training room and saw his teacher staring out the window, his back to him.

"Mr. Tillman?" Trace asked. "You wanted to talk?"

Mr. Tillman was probably the most athletic teacher at the school. He had a bald, shiny head, rippling muscles, and one of those faces that made him look permanently angry. There was a rumor about him that he used to do underground cage fighting before he decided to calm down and become a teacher.

When Mr. Tillman turned and faced Trace, he had his sunglasses on. Trace thought nothing of it. He just assumed it was going to be a quick conversation because Mr. Tillman was ready to head out for the day.

"Hello, Trace, how are you doing today?" he asked, his arms still crossed but casually.

"Fine?"

Mr. Tillman had never asked him that before.

"Yeah? Are you sure you're not... stressed? Are you sure you haven't been dealing with... a lot lately?"

"How would you know?" Trace asked. "Who's talking about me to you?"

Leave it to even the teachers to gossip about his breakup with Amberly.

"No one talks to me about you personally," Mr. Tillman said. "But then again, no one here knows who I really am."

Trace raised an eyebrow, completely confused. What was the point of this? Why was he here? He looked around. There was still nobody else in the room with them. Outside, the halls sounded pretty empty. Mr. Tillman's classroom was located in the back of the school, near the gymnasium. All of the students were likely mostly outside by now, on the curb of the front of the school, waiting for their parents to pick them up, saying goodbye to their friends, or running to catch the bus.

Trace was about to ask Mr. Tillman what the heck he was talking about, but then Mr. Tillman removed his sunglasses.

Instead of the normal brown eyes Trace was used to seeing, there were sockets of fire.

"Rezin." Trace should have known. He felt like an idiot. This was a setup. He had been so distracted by what happened with Amberly today that he hadn't even considered that something like this could happen. For just a moment, he had felt like a normal teenage boy dealing with his normal teenage problems, and he had completely forgotten that he had much, much bigger things going on.

And he was defenseless. He didn't even have his sword. It wasn't exactly easy to take places; it stuck out of his backpack. If he got caught with it here, he'd likely get suspended or expelled because having weapons on campus was heavily forbidden. Amberly's gauntlet was large, but it was just small enough to fit in her book bag. Kire's book was obviously easy to carry around—people probably assumed he checked it out from the library. Kaos got away with wearing that crown on his head, even if it was a little strange. People didn't question it because he was so popular. And Rose had that pendant she wore around her neck. It already looked like something she would wear normally. He doubted anyone even paid it any attention.

Rezin must have known he would be the one most likely to not have anything to fight with.

And now Trace knew he was in deep, deep trouble.

Rezin, who had either taken over Mr. Tillman's body or disguised himself to look like Mr. Tillman, let out a burning laugh. He was terrifying. And Mr. Tillman already looked terrifying without flaming eyes flaming sockets for eyes.

Trace turned to bolt out of there, but Rezin was quicker. He disappeared into thin air and then reappeared right in front of the exit of the room.

Trace picked up a weighted disc and flung it at Rezin. Rezin dodged it, and it flew into the door, cracking the glass.

Trace tried to run out again, but Rezin used his powers to pull Trace back to the middle of the room, where he tripped over a workout bench and fell on his back.

Use what you've got, he told himself, ignoring the pain, lunging quickly for the barbell resting on the chest press machine. It was long, much longer than he preferred, and it weighed forty pounds without any added weights on it, but still, Trace turned it vertically, like a sword or a bat, and was so quick to act that he managed to land a hit right into Rezin's side.

Rezin flew into the Smith machine and yelled. Then, he welded his magic in between his hands. His ball of light sucked the electricity out of the room, making the lights overhead spark, and Trace ducked. The ball of electric mass soared over him, missing him by centimeters, sizzling some of his hair, and instead hit the white-painted brick wall.

"Why do you even want to fight us anymore?" Trace managed to yell out. "Yash can't come here! We closed the portal! He can't get to us! Just give up already!"

Rezin didn't offer to say anything back. He used some sort of telepathic ability, like Amberly had, to lift a fifty-pound dumbbell in the air and send it hurling toward him.

It bashed into Trace's stomach and knocked him off his feet with such force he was blasted into a punching bag, and he groaned as he fell to the ground. The lights were still flickering like crazy overhead. Rezin was drawing more electricity from them. He was going to kill Trace with the next blast. Trace was sure of it.

Then suddenly, the door to the room flew open, and at first, Trace figured Rezin did it with his mind. But then he saw none other than Rose standing in the doorway, a fearful expression on her pale face.

"Mr. Harrison!" she screamed down the hallway. "Come quick!"

That was all she needed to do. Drawing attention to Rezin

would expose him for what he was, so in an instant, Rezin vanished, leaving Trace in pain, crumpled on the floor.

Rose raced into the room to help him to his feet. He moaned in pain some more.

"Are you all right?" she asked.

"Where is Mr. Harrison?" Trace asked, worried the teacher was going to come in and see the mess it looked like Trace had made all on his own.

"He wasn't really out there," Rose said, shaking her head quickly. "I just wanted to make Rezin think that a teacher was nearby."

Trace clutched his stomach. "How did you know I was in here?"

"I was in the greenhouse. I could see the lights in here flashing all weird and crazy while I was watering one of the plants. I just had a feeling it wasn't anything good."

"Yeah. Thanks for coming."

"We should get you some ice or something."

"I'll be fine."

"Will you, though?" Rose asked. Trace stared at her, sensing she was asking him something *else*. She continued, "We saw the breakup."

Trace rolled his eyes. "It's whatever."

"No, it's not," Rose said, reading him like a book.

"Don't worry, I won't let it interfere with the defeating Rezin."

"I don't care about that. You guys were together for a long time. I just want to make sure that you're okay."

Rose was always so sweet. Trace hated that he had ever been so mean to her. But he could tell exactly why Amberly chose to continue to dislike her. She probably resented Rose for being able to be nice to people. It was a quality Amberly severely lacked.

"I appreciate it, Rose, but we have other things to focus on right now."

She nodded. Trace continued clutching his stomach, which was throbbing. He had already been injured there before Rezin threw the weight into him. It had happened when he was fighting back in the Albus realm. He lifted his shirt just to see how bad the damage was now, and before he could even get a good look, Rose was gasping.

"That looks bad!"

But the old injury he sustained during their fight in Albus realm was already almost gone, replaced by a fresh bruising red mark where the weight hit him. As The Unlikely Defenders, they healed much, much quicker than the average person.

"I'll be back to normal in no time."

Rose sighed. "I know it's probably the last thing you want to do, but we should really get everyone together and tell them what happened. Rezin attacked *at school*. He's infiltrated the teachers. He can be anyone at any time. And he doesn't care what kind of mess he makes. He has to be stopped."

Great. It looked like Trace was going to have to see Amberly again today after all.

7

The gang all met up together at Aunt Marg's, their usual gathering spot. Aunt Marg's was a grocery store with a large room in the back for having tea and treats. The place looked like something right out of the Albus realm, and the Albus realm looked like something right out of a fairytale. The tea room had a large clock on the wall with tea cups instead of numbers. There was a large wooden shelf with different painted ceramic teapots that had knitted covers around them. The tables were clothed in soft, plaid pastel colors with frilly trimmings, and people like Trace looked like they did not belong when they sat down at a dainty table.

"You need to make this quick," Trace grumbled as he watched Amberly walk through the door to join them. Just the sight of her made him nauseated. And it didn't help that his stomach was already in a lot of pain from what had just happened with Rezin. "I would really rather be anywhere else right now."

"What is this about?" Amberly snapped at the others when she sat down. "Is it really that important that you're forcing me to be near *him*?"

The "him" she was referring to was very obviously Trace. Trace wasn't the only one who was still fuming over their incident in the hallway earlier.

"I know things are weird and awkward right now," Rose said, surprising Trace with how she was the one to lead this meeting. She usually hung back on the sidelines, chiming in only when she needed to.

"You got that right," Kaos said, his arms crossed. He wasn't looking at any of them. He touched the crown on his head, and in seconds, Aunt Marg was coming into the room smiling brightly and telling them that she would be right back with their tea and treats and that it was all on the house today. Then she disappeared quickly.

"You made her do that, didn't you?" Kire asked Kaos.

All Kaos did was smile.

"Kaos!" Rose complained. "That's not right!"

Kaos merely shrugged. She shot him a dirty look and then continued on.

"Anyway. Rezin disguised himself as Mr. Tillman today and attacked Trace. Things could've ended badly if I hadn't found him. He got really hurt."

"I'm fine," Trace was quick to throw in.

Rose ignored him. "What is the plan, you guys? "

"We need to figure out a way to kill Rezin, that's for sure," Kire said. "But we also left the Albus realm a huge mess. Yes, we were just trying to protect their world and save everyone, but we left destruction in our path every time we defeated another one of Yash's minions. I think we have a responsibility to make things right."

"I agree," Rose said. "And we need to talk to Albus's wife."

"Joy," Amberly grumbled.

"Maybe we'll learn something from someone in the Albus realm that will give us insight into how to go about killing Rezin here," Kaos chimed in. Then Aunt Marg returned with their tea and dish of cookies, and she smiled pleasantly and sat everything down on the table. "Whatever else you need, I am at your service!" she said, beaming at all of them.

Rose glared at Kaos until Aunt Marg left again.

"Stop doing that," she demanded. But Kaos just smiled again.

"The mind controller has a good point," Kire said. "I think the answers we're looking for are not found here on Earth."

"But The White Forest is on fire," Trace brought up. "How are we supposed to get back to the portal?"

"I know The White Forest better than maybe anyone in Montgomery," Rose said. "I will track the fire, and then I will map out a way for us to get back to the portal without getting caught in it. I'll let you guys know as soon as I figure it out."

8

Trace, relying on Rose to figure out a plan for them to get back to the portal into the Albus realm, went home after their meeting at Aunt Marg's. Kaos drove everyone except for Amberly, who didn't take Kaos's offer to be dropped off at her aunt's. She dashed out of there as soon as their meeting adjourned, not saying anything to anyone, her nose sticking up in the air because she was Amberly, and she was always snooty like that.

It had been a trying and tiring day for Trace. All he wanted to do was go home, attempt to get some homework done—just enough so that he wouldn't fail and have to repeat his junior year—and then go to sleep after a long hot shower.

When he was dropped off at his house, the sky behind it was still glowing orange from the fire in The White Forest. It was a constant reminder of what he had caused. What if the forest was burnt to nothing? What if smoke filled everyone's lungs and caused lots of health problems later on? What if he, by trying to save people from dying, ultimately ended up killing people instead?

He shook the thought away and walked to his front door. Inside the house, his mother was in her usual spot on the sofa with the TV on, but the second Trace saw her, he was almost alarmed because of how sick she looked. Her eyes were so sunken in, and her skin was so pasty. She was getting so thin, too.

"Hi, Mom," Trace said, trying to keep his exhaustion out of his tone.

"T-Trace," she said with a hiccup. She sat up and grabbed the glass from the coffee table. There was a dark red liquid inside of it. She took a sip and then sat back, looking unsteady even though she was sitting.

"Maybe you should just stick to some water," Trace tried. He hadn't even stepped away from the entryway, a little tiled space by the door that had a small table with a catchall tray on it and a mirror hanging above it, yet.

"Have you gotten money for my meds yet?" she asked slowly instead of acknowledging his comment.

"I promise I'm working on it." It wasn't fair that this all fell on Trace. How much more stress could he handle? "I have to do some homework. Are you going to be all right?"

She sighed heavily and nodded her head. Then she resumed drinking from the glass.

Trace walked into the kitchen and set his bag on the small breakfast table. He pulled out what he needed, grabbed a giant glass of milk and a couple of snacks from the pantry, and then sat down to get started.

He found it increasingly harder to concentrate on his school-work when, every so often, his mother kept returning to the kitchen with her empty glass, only to refill it with more of the dark red liquid. Trace was uncomfortable with the fact that she was opening her third bottle of the day.

"You're so smart, you know that?" she told him as she nearly overflowed her glass. "My son doesn't need to do stupid homework. Homework doesn't make anyone any smarter. Imagine if *we* had to go to work all day long and then come home and keep working! Ridiculous."

"Thanks, Mom," Trace said, rolling his eyes, but his back was to his mother, who was in the kitchen, so she didn't see it. Trace did not think he was at all intelligent. He was nothing compared to Kaos. Kaos had all the brains. So did Kire, too.

"You got your smartness from me," his mother said. "Not from your idiotic father."

"Mom, I don't want to talk about him," Trace was quick to say. If his mom started talking about their father when she was in… a state such as this… it was nearly impossible to get her to stop, and things quickly often started to spiral.

"Not talking about him isn't going to make him stop existing," his mother replied, suddenly a bit of an edge to her voice.

"I didn't say that," Trace said.

"Your father—"

"Mom, I have homework," Trace interrupted.

"I don't care!"

He turned around in his chair and finally looked his mother in the eye. She had to hold herself up against the countertop. At this point, Trace couldn't tell if it was because of the drinking or because of her illness. If she kept on like this, she was going to die, and Trace was going to be left with no one.

Sighing, not wanting to get into this with her, he stood up and began packing up his stuff.

"What are you doing?" his mother asked, her words slurring.

"I'm just—I forgot that Kaos wanted to work on a school project together," Trace lied. But he knew he could go to Kaos's. It didn't matter what time of day it was. Trace was always welcome there.

"Great, so you're leaving?" His mother resumed drinking from her new glass.

On the inside, Trace was shaking with anger. It took a lot for him to not burst out yelling at her. The only thing that stopped him was thoughts of his father—how he would do the same thing. And how much it tortured his mother when it happened. Trace would never forget the terrified expression on her face, placed there by his father over and over again. And Trace didn't want to do that to her, no matter how angry he felt.

"I'm sorry," Trace managed to say. "I'll try to hurry." He didn't at all mean it. If anything, he was going to try and stay at Kaos's as long as possible. Maybe he'd even stay the night there, and hopefully, his mom would be sober when he returned in the morning.

"I was going to throw a frozen lasagna in the oven for us. But whatever. More for me," Vivian replied.

"That's fine. I'm sure there will be something to eat over there."

He threw his backpack on and then walked into the kitchen to kiss his mother on the cheek. Just one simple, light peck, and still, she nearly fell over.

"Mom, come sit down." He helped her—as she carried her stupid drink—back over to the sofa and got her seated.

She sipped from the glass and smiled at him.

"I wish you would stop this," Trace whispered, his hands still on her shoulders and his body bent over her. He said the words, knowing full well that she wouldn't remember them in the morning.

"I wish life wasn't so painful," his mother deadpanned. "Then maybe I could."

It would have been much faster just to get Kaos to come to pick him up, but Trace took the back way to his friend's house anyway, bringing his Pentfire with him so that he could practice with it in the cover of alleyways and behind bushes.

Kaos's house looked like it didn't even belong in Montgomery. It was too monstrous. More fit for Beverly Hills—not that Trace had ever been there. It was one of those houses that had an entryway like a hotel with a big circular driveway that the roof hung over in front of the front door. There was also a massive, green front lawn where he and Kaos had spent hours practicing soccer drills. The mansion was built in the '90s, but the architect had clearly known how to construct it to where, so many years later, it would still look practically brand new.

Trace stuck his sword in his backpack, the handle sticking out, and rang the doorbell instead of knocking because the front door had this massive iron covering over the frosted glass, and knocking on it wouldn't have been loud enough to reach the furthest points of the house.

As much as Trace liked Kaos's parents, he was glad when Kaos answered instead of them. He wasn't in the mood to be polite to them. He wasn't really in the mood to be polite to anybody.

"Oh man, your mom again?" Kaos guessed, just by reading the look on Trace's face. And the fact that he had showed up unannounced again. "Or is it the breakup?"

Trace basically pushed way inside Kaos's house, not waiting for permission. "I don't want to talk about it," he said as he went.

"Fine by me," Kaos replied, shutting the door behind him. It was so heavy that when it clicked shut, it sounded as loud as if he had slammed a regular wooden door.

They walked through the massive, opulent, tastefully decorated house, over to where there were two winding staircases flanking the same balcony of the second story. They each took their own staircase and raced up, something they had been doing for years, and this time, Kaos beat him even though Trace was usually always the winner.

"Dang, you *must* be in a mood," Kaos commented as they resumed the walk to his bedroom.

"Dude." Trace's voice was warning-like.

Kaos held his hands up in surrender. "My bad. Won't bring it up again."

Kaos's bedroom, like the rest of the house, was incredible. It was large enough to fit a king-size bed, and it had its own bathroom. There was a walk-in closet as well, filled to the brim with neatly organized clothing, all in a shade of black, in true Kaos fashion.

The decor in the room was rather dark as well. But academic, like Trace had just stepped into an evil professor's Albus. There were dark, wood-paneled walls, except one was composed of wooden bookcases overflowing with things Trace would never have any desire to read and wasn't sure he'd understand even if he tried. Instead of carpeting, Kaos had a wooden floor. The shades that hung over his window were controlled by a remote, and the TV he had mounted on the wall above his dresser was larger than the TV Trace had in his living room.

"So, what do you want to do?" Kaos asked.

"Don't you still have homework, too?" Trace replied.

"Already finished it."

"How?"

Kaos shrugged. "I did a lot of it in class. And it was easy."

"Great. Then you can help me with mine." Trace sat down at Kaos's desk, which had an insane gaming computer set up on it, and Kaos flopped down on his bed. Together, they worked on Trace's homework, but it didn't take long for Kaos to get very, very bored.

"Hey, do you wanna see something cool?" Kaos asked.

"What?" Trace turned around in Kaos's desk chair to look at him.

Kaos reached to his nightstand and put his crown on his head. Then he squinted his eyes a bit as if he was concentrating, and within a handful of seconds, there was a knock on his bedroom door.

"Kaos," his mother, Betty, said with a bright smile on her face as she poked her head in. "What do you want for dinner? I want to make your favorite."

"Trace and I would like some good steaks," Kaos answered smartly.

"Coming right up, my darling boy. And hi, Trace."

"Hi, Mrs. Miles."

When Betty, a dark-haired beauty who did not look old enough to have a teenage son and always wore business attire, closed the door, Kaos grinned at Trace.

"Isn't it great? I've been getting so much better at using my crown. I can literally do whatever I want."

"So, you're making her cook us a steak dinner?"

"Yep."

Trace smiled weakly and shook his head. He thought maybe that was all Kaos had wanted to show him, but then a minute later, there was another knock on the door, and his father entered the bedroom, holding a small stack of papers in his hand. Roald Miles stood before Kao's bed, seeming as if he didn't even realize Trace was in the room with them.

"Finished with all your homework. And I made sure everything is one hundred percent correct and not plagiarized."

"Thanks, Father. You can set it on my nightstand."

Roald obeyed him. And it was so strange to see. Mr. Miles was a nice guy, but he was also a very successful businessman—the type of guy who didn't do anything for anyone.

"Oh, and hi, Trace," Roald said when he turned to leave and noticed Trace at the desk.

"Hi, Mr. Miles."

When he was gone, Trace glared at Kaos. "So you *didn't* do your homework in class."

"I wasn't going to show you that much, but I couldn't resist. Isn't it great?"

"Sure, Kaos. I'm glad it's working for you."

Not wanting to start any more drama, Trace didn't say what he was truly thinking about what he just witnessed Kaos doing with his powers. He didn't think it was right to manipulate his own parents. He didn't think it was right to manipulate *anybody* he cared about.

But Kaos did what Kaos wanted. And that's always how it was.

Trace had been hoping for some great distraction when he arrived at school the next day. Something to make him think about anything other than his breakup with Amberly and the way his mother had behaved last night.

But he had not been expecting a distraction like this.

A girl in their class, Annabel, appeared almost out of nowhere as Trace walked to his locker.

"Hi, Trace," she said, practically bouncing on her heels. Annabel was a sweetheart. Everyone seemed to like her. She was very short, possibly the shortest girl at their high school, but Trace was pretty sure it only added to her charm. She was cute, with red hair, green eyes and millions of freckles. Cute, but not hot. Not supermodel status like Amberly was.

"Hey, Annabel," Trace said, thinking it was weird that she had approached him.

"I'm so sorry about what happened to you and Amberly," she said.

Trace itched the back of his neck. "Oh, it's all right."

"I think you made the right choice, though," she said.

This took him by surprise. "You... do?"

She flashed him a smile and looked up at him underneath her eyelashes.

Was Annabel flirting with him?

"Most definitely," she said. "Amberly is evil. And controlling. You don't need that. You deserve a good girl."

She may as well have winked at him and pointed at herself.

"Hmm... Thank you, I guess," he said. This conversation felt awkward. Strange. Trace wasn't used to being flirted with by other girls. Mainly because Amberly would have rung their necks if they did. But now, Amberly was no longer in the picture. Now, it was suddenly safe again for other girls to talk to him.

As Annabel practically skipped away, Trace stared after her, wondering if maybe he had imagined that entire conversation. He rubbed his eyes, and then the school bell rang, and he made his way to class.

But even just walking through the hall, Trace was noticing something he hadn't really ever paid attention to before. The stares. So many people were staring at him, and most of those people were female. They stood clustered together in their cliques, gazing at him and whispering in each other's ears. And when he got to class, girls sitting by themselves at their desks followed him with their eyes as he sat down in his.

And it went on like this all day. When the students needed to pair up to work on worksheets, random chicks asked Trace to be his partner. When he took a bathroom pass in the middle of one of his classes, he ran into a senior girl in the hallway who smiled at him flirtatiously and gave him a wave. At lunch, he stood behind two girls in the lunch line who didn't realize he was there, and he overheard them gossiping about him, talking about how excited they were that Trace Henderson was now single. Apparently, he was St. Bernard High's most eligible bachelor. It surprised Trace to hear it. He knew he was good-looking, and he knew he was very well-built, but Kaos was also handsome, *and* he had brains. Didn't girls prefer that?

Still, Trace continued getting strange new attention from people he didn't normally talk to all the way until the last class of the day. They had a bit of free time before the bell rang because Ms. Wright had finished everything she wanted to say. So Tatum Blanchard, one of his classmates, approached him and gave him yet another flirty smile. "I am excited to see you win after school today."

Trace looked behind him, wondering if maybe she was speaking to somebody else. However, no one else was there. So, he turned back to her. Her brown eyes looked slightly devilish as she tucked her dyed blue hair behind her ears.

"Win *what*?" he asked.

"Your fight," she said.

"Fight?"

"You're such a goof." Tatum giggled and playfully nudged him with her fist. "I'll be cheering for you." She didn't even wait for Trace to ask her to further explain herself before she returned to her friends in the corner of the room and started giggling with them.

Trace turned around to go find Kaos, but Kire and Rose were closer, and they were staring at him pointedly.

"Do you have any idea what she was talking about?" Trace asked.

"How do you not know?" Kire asked. "Apparently, a fight has been set up for after school today. You and Carter McDuffie."

Carter McDuffie was only a sophomore. But Trace supposed he had heard that the kid was always looking for a fight. He was a troublemaker. A rebel.

"That would've been nice to know a long time ago," Trace said irritably, glaring at Kaos even though Kaos was too busy having a discussion with Ms. Wright to see him.

"I suppose it's got to be pretty distracting with all the attention you've been receiving now that you're single," Rose said. She looked almost annoyed. But Trace didn't understand why.

"You got that right," he told her. Then he leaned closer and began whispering to them so others wouldn't hear. "Ever since the news spread that I am single, chicks won't leave me alone."

"Yeah, meanwhile, Amberly is getting harassed and treated like Satan's spawn by everyone," Rose said.

"Hey, I don't have any part of that," Trace said, holding his hands up in surrender. "Yesterday, I could have sworn everyone was on *her* side. But today, even her cheerleading friends are giving me flirty looks, I swear. They're pretending to be on her side, but they're completely faking it."

"Of course they're faking it," Kire said. "They're cheerleaders."

"Watch it," Trace snapped, so used to coming to Amberly's defense. "Amberly is a cheerleader, too."

"Yeah," Kire continued anyway. "And she can be pretty fake, too. I am allowed to say it; she *is* my sister."

Beside him, Rose giggled.

"I didn't want to end things with Amberly," Trace admitted. "It only makes things more difficult with... everything going on. But she made it happen."

"You really think you'll stay broken up?" Kire asked, suddenly looking as if this was his first time hearing about them even breaking up in the first place.

"I..." Trace was unsure how to respond. Could things get better with Amberly? Could they resolve their issues and pretend like the breakup never happened? Or were they really, truly never speaking again unless it had to do with the quintets?

Before he could answer, the final bell rang, and Kaos threw his arm around Trace's shoulder and steered him away from Kire and Rose before saying, "My friend, we have a fight to go prepare for."

10

Not long ago, Trace Henderson would have been thrilled to hear news of Kaos finding him another victim to terrorize. It had always been an easy way to get money because Trace never lost. And Trace never liked to back down from a fight. In fact, he *liked* them. He liked the feeling of his fist connecting with flesh. Of causing somebody else pain. He liked being able to release his anger. He liked feeling powerful and on top of the world.

A short while ago, if you had ever asked Trace if he would change his mind about the way he felt about fighting for money or fighting in general, he would have never imagined himself feeling the way he did now.

Trace didn't want to have this fight with Carter McDuffie. It felt... empty. Pointless. Impractical. But as he mentally prepared himself for it after school, he knew that it wasn't pointless. He knew that it would get him money because Kaos organized it to where everyone had to pay if they wanted to see it. It was risky, and if he was caught, he would surely be expelled, but how else was Trace going to get money? It wasn't an easy thing to come by. And he had a gift. An ability to win. What else was he good at that could make him money? Trace truly felt he didn't have any other talents he could put to use.

But at the same time, he didn't have this pent-up urge to fight people like Carter McDuffie. Not when he had his Pentfire and had all of those minions of Yash's to defeat in the Albus realm. Not when he had gotten the opportunity to fight and end Heno and Jago. Although Trace had been having a rough time of it lately with his mother and Amberly, he wasn't looking for some outlet to release his anger anymore. And he wondered what that meant when it came to doing the actual fighting.

The fight was going to be held just off school campus. To prepare for it, Trace was in the school's waiting room, pumping iron and trying to get himself angry. He was like the Hulk when he was angry: he was so much stronger.

He was annoyed that he learned from that blue-haired chick, Tatum, that he was even having a fight. That he had gone all day long without even knowing it was about to happen. Kaos hadn't said a word to him. But at the same time, Trace knew he shouldn't be upset with Kaos—he was only trying to help. He was only acting as he always had. And Trace was going to be getting a decent amount of money out of it. Enough to finally swing by and pick up his mom's prescription on his way home. That was the only aspect of the fight that he was looking forward to.

When the door to the weight room opened, Trace growled and dropped his dumbbells to the ground with loud thuds. He was irritated to no longer have the weight room to himself, and he was going to be really irritated if it was his weights class teacher, Mr. Tillman, back to attack him again because he was still really Rezin in disguise.

He turned around, waiting, ready to snap at the intruder and tell them to buzz off, but he stopped short, his mouth hanging open, when he saw the plant-loving girl in the weights room once again.

"Rose?"

Rose was standing before him in a way so familiar to how Amberly liked to stand that it was off-putting to Trace. Her arms were crossed. She had one hip jutted out. She was tapping her foot against the rubber flooring, and her eyes seemed to be ablaze.

"Trace, what are you doing?" she asked, her voice flat.

"What do you mean?" Trace asked. "I'm working out."

She rolled her eyes. "No. I'm not talking about right now. I'm talking about this fight. With Carter McDuffie."

"Oh. McDuffie."

Sure, Trace liked Rose enough. They had had some good talks. She was a good person. But who did she think she was, coming in here and thinking she had any sort of say over the decisions Trace was making?

"You wouldn't understand, Rose," he continued. "Now, if you'll excuse me, I really need to finish this set."

"No."

"I'm sorry?"

"Trace, don't do it."

"Why do you care so much about Carter McDuffie?"

"I don't care about Carter McDuffie. I've never even talked to him before. It's not about him. It's about the principle of it all. A fight ring? For money? I just don't get it. Trace, you have your"—she looked around to make sure nobody else was in the room before looking back at him—"Pentfire. Your sword. You're supposed to fight by defeating Yash's minions. By protecting people. Not hurting them. I thought you had changed."

"Look, I would prefer to be doing it that way; you're right. But I can't just..." Trace trailed off because he didn't want to tell her too much. Rose didn't need to know why he needed this money. He didn't need the pity.

"Are you afraid to tell Kaos no or something?" she asked, trying to guess. "He's not that scary, Trace. You don't have to do everything he says. You're not his puppet."

"I know that!" Trace yelled, his voice suddenly thundering in the otherwise empty room.

It shook Rose slightly, like she hadn't been expecting the outburst. But Trace didn't blame her. He hadn't been expecting to get so angry so quickly.

He began trying to apologize. "Rose, I..."

Instead of being angry, Rose just looked hurt. "I hope you at least consider what I've asked," she said before quickly leaving Trace alone again.

"Crap," Trace said under his breath, feeling bad for upsetting her. Maybe he should have just told her the real reason why he was doing this. Maybe she would have understood more and wouldn't have pitied him like he expected.

He picked up his dumbbells to resume his bicep curls, but then the sound of the door opening *again* made him drop them a second time.

This time, it was Kaos entering the room.

"What were you doing talking with Rose?" Kaos asked, pointing behind him. "I just passed her in the hall. She looked angry. Wouldn't even say anything to me."

"Long story."

Kaos shrugged. Truly, nothing bothered him. Ever. "You about ready? People have started to gather, and I've already collected a good amount of cash. So it has to happen."

"Nice of you to tell me that it *was* happening," Trace grumbled.

"I thought I did," he said simply. "Either way, Carter might have a lot of experience fighting, but he still doesn't have the muscles that you do, my guy. I think you've got this in the bag."

"I really don't feel like doing this," Trace admitted, shocking even himself. Now that the words were out, he kept going. "Can't we just give everyone their money back? Find some other way to make the cash? I'm sick of doing this, dude."

"Was it something Rose said?" Kaos asked, his eyes turning dark.

"No." Trace had already been having all those thoughts before

Rose came in.

"Trace. This fight has to happen. Everyone is expecting it. And it's easy money. Because it's an easy win. You're good at fighting. You beat everyone."

"Yeah, but I do enough fighting trying to protect this world."

"But that doesn't pay for your mom's medicine."

"I know. Which is why I want to find another way."

Kaos put a hand on Trace's shoulder. "Look. We can try to think of other ways to make the cash. But that has to happen *after* this fight, got it? It's too late now. You know your mom needs her meds, Trace. Before it gets bad."

Trace thought of how sick his mom had looked yesterday. Of how she continued her drinking anyway. Kaos was right. They could look for other ways to make the money for her medication, but how long would it take for them to find another way? If he didn't do this fight today, he might not see money for a couple more weeks. And by then, what would his mom's health status be? Trace saw how much Amberly's mom's death affected her. He couldn't let that happen to him, too.

"Fine," Trace said, glowering. "Just get it over with then."

"Attaboy."

And so the lion tamer led the way of his lion to the circle in the dirt that had been created by the mass of students waiting to see the fight unfold between Carter McDuffie and Trace Henderson.

"Where is he?" Trace asked Kaos. They were in the center of the circle now, and everyone's excited voices were so loud that no one could directly hear what it was Trace and Kaos were discussing.

"He should be here any second," Kaos said.

Just as Trace was hoping maybe he would be a no-show, the crowd parted, and Carter McDuffie entered the circle. He was leaner than Trace, somewhere in between his build and Kaos's gangly one. It was still clear because of the tank top he was wearing, even though it was cold out, that Carter had strong muscles. And he was wearing sunglasses, so Trace couldn't correctly gauge his expression. His mouth was unmoving as he stood on the other side of the circle and faced him.

Trace found himself scanning the crowd, looking for the person who always had his back, who was always cheering for him and only him. But instead of finding Amberly anywhere, he met eyes with a sorrowful Rose. She was silently pleading for him not to do this.

But I have to do this, Trace thought.

"I'm ready," he said to Kaos, tearing his eyes away from Rose.

Kaos beamed around at the crowd. "My fellow classmates," he said loudly. And once Kaos was speaking, everybody stopped to listen to him. "Let the fight... commence!"

Wanting to just get this over with, Trace made the first move, advancing on Carter and swinging a fist. He wanted to catch him by surprise with how quickly he moved.

However, Carter had apparently been anticipating that. He blocked the punch with his forearm, and just the block had been strong enough to cause Trace's fist to throb.

Growling, Trace threw another punch, but again it was blocked. Wanting to leave Carter no time to make his own move, Trace just kept, punch after punch, trying to land one somewhere on his body.

How was Carter fast enough to stop him? How did it seem he was anticipating all of his moves? And why was he wearing sunglasses when there was a risk of him getting punched in the face?

Just as Carter threw his first punch, one that Trace couldn't block before it flew into his cheek, Trace realized the truth.

It wasn't Carter McDuffie before him.

This was Rezin. The glasses were the giveaway, covering his fiery eyeballs. Was he possessing Carter? Or did he just make himself look like Carter and the real Carter was stuck in a closet somewhere? Was the real Carter still alive? Was the real Mr. Tillman still alive?

What had Rezin done?

New feelings of anger flooded Trace's body, weighing him down and grounding him in this new reality. And the new reality was that by having this fight right now, Trace *was* doing his part in protecting the world. He wasn't just some high school kid trying to get some extra cash by taking others down. He was an Unlikely Defender of Earth, trying to prevent this evil being from causing death, pain, and destruction.

Trace yelled, his body feeling like one of those strength games at a carnival where you hit the puck with a hammer and try to make the bell ring. With Rezin's punch, the puck had been hit, and Trace's yell was the bell.

He fought harder. For a moment, he didn't understand why Rezin didn't just use his powers, but then he quickly figured it was because there were too many witnesses. Too many people would learn the truth of there being other entities in this universe. So Rezin was trying to really play the part of a normal teenage boy.

And *while* Trace fought harder, Rezin fought skillfully. He was quick to dodge. Quick to block. He knew when he had an opening to throw a punch at Trace. People started cheering less for Trace and more for Carter.

Bunch of bandwagoners, Trace thought to himself as his head pounded and he swallowed a mouthful of blood.

He couldn't believe this was happening. Trace never lost a fight against a student. And even though Carter wasn't actually a student, his classmates at St. Bernard High would never know it.

What would happen to his reputation?

What would people say?

Where was the real Carter McDuffie?

His thoughts overwhelming him, and his desperation to protect himself, ended up being Trace's downfall.

With one final blow, the lights were completely knocked out of him, and everything went black.

11

When Trace eventually came to, he didn't want to open his eyes, so they remained closed. He was embarrassed, unable to believe that he actually lost a fight. In front of the *entire* school. Of course, he had been fighting Rezin, but it wasn't as if all of his classmates knew that. To them, they all thought he lost a fight against a *sophomore*. Trace knew he was never going to be able to live it down. This made him hate Rezin more than he ever had before.

"I'll give it thirty more seconds, and if he doesn't wake up, we need to call 911," Rose's voice said, and Trace assumed she was talking to the other members of The Unlikely Defenders. He didn't know how long he had been unconscious or where they even were anymore. Perhaps they carried him off somewhere? As he listened closer, he could still hear other voices in the background. It sounded as if his peers were somewhere in the distance, talking excitedly with each other, maybe congratulating the winner of the fight.

"Rose, I know you're worried, but remember, he has super healing powers. He'll be back in no time." That was Kaos's voice.

Kaos.

Trace was also mad at him. Enough so that he was able to open his eyes and peek around at everyone. He had been right; the only ones around him were Kaos, Kire, and Rose. There was no Amberly. None of the girls from earlier who had been excited for him to win the fight. It was as if since he lost, nobody was interested in him anymore. And it felt low. He was unable to see that the ones who mattered most, besides Amberly, were right in front of him.

"He's awake!" Kire gasped, hitting the others so that they paid attention. Everyone looked down at him, and Trace sat himself up, his head throbbing as well as other various body parts that Rezin had attacked. He wondered what he looked like. How bad it was. Was he going to have to hide anything from his mom? She would lose it if she knew how he was getting money for her medicine. The last thing Vivian wanted was for Trace to be like his father.

"That was Rezin," Trace informed the others. "It wasn't a fair fight."

"Don't worry, Trace, we know," Kire replied.

"I knew it instantly," Rose added.

Trace shook his head, still angry with himself even though beating a fight against Rezin, all by himself, not able to use his Pentfire, was obviously impossible. Trace was just almost incapable of not being hard on himself.

"I was set up to fail," he said, glaring at Kaos. As he sat there on the ground in pain, the other three stood crouching around him. He growled; he could see in the distance that he had been right—everyone who had paid to watch the fight was gathered around the new top dog at their high school.

But where was the real Carter McDuffie, anyway? Was he inside Rezin still? Or did Rezin kill him or kidnap him and steal his form? None of them knew how similar Rezin was to Jago or Heno. Rezin was a whole other ball game when it came to the things he could do. No wonder he was Yash's top minion.

"Dude, I had no idea," Kaos said to Trace. "It was an oversight I should've looked into. Especially with what happened with Mr. Tillman. But, hey, win or lose, you still got paid for the fight."

And obviously, this was important. Trace hadn't even wanted to do the fight at all. But he *did* need that money. He held out his hand, and Kaos put a fat stack of bills in it.

"Don't spend it all in one place," Rose said with an eye roll.

If she only knew, Trace thought.

They gave Trace a couple more minutes to stop feeling so dizzy, then they helped him to his feet and went back to Kaos's car. The whole walk over, Trace looked around for any signs of his ex-girlfriend, thinking that it felt strange to not have her with them. But she was nowhere in sight. It was a good *and* bad thing—at least he didn't see her over-celebrating Carter McDuffie/Rezin's win. Could she tell that he had been fighting Rezin? Did she have any idea?

Trace sat in the front seat, not buckling himself in because his body hurt too badly, and stared out the window. After the loss, he didn't feel much like talking. The loss of Amberly. The loss of the fight.

"Oh, by the way, Trace," Kire piped up from the backseat, leaning forward and sticking his face in between the two front ones. "We talked while you were... trying to stay alive against Rezin. It's happening tonight."

"What is?" Trace grumbled.

"We're waiting until it gets super late. Then we're going into The White Forest," he says.

Trace looked out the window in the direction of The White Forest, where the smoke was still billowing. The fire was still roaring. It was dangerous. But the fire was also his fault. "Are we going to battle the fires?" he asked.

"We'll do what we can on our way," Rose said, "but we really have to focus on avoiding firefighters and making it to the portal... unharmed. We're going back into the Albus realm to start some cleanup."

"And what about Amberly? Is she going to come?" Trace asked. He thought he sounded both bitter and hopeful at the same time.

"I'm going to talk to her," Kaos announced. "Since I am the only one she seems to really want to be around right now."

Trace slouched in his seat and didn't say another word for the remainder of the car ride.

After Kaos dropped him off at home, he had to pull his phone out and turn his front-facing camera on to get a look at his injuries.

Crud. He had quite the shiner on his right eye.

Not wanting his mom to see it, he threw his hoodie up over his head and pulled it as far over his face as it would go. Then he entered his house.

"Hey, Mom," he said in a rushed tone. As usual, she was on the couch. "You've got medicine for today, right? I can pick up more tomorrow. I have the money." He didn't look at her as he spoke. He was walking away from her toward the hall leading to his room.

"Oh, hi, honey," she said in a slow, drawn-out voice. "Where are you going?"

"I was at the gym for a long time after school, and I am seriously sweating and disgusting," he lied. "I need to just hop in the shower. Trust me, you don't wanna come near me." He stood lingering in the darkness of the hallway. Over his shoulder, he could see his mom squinting in his direction, unable to fully make him out.

"All right," she said. "Well, thank you, Trace. Yes, I'll be good for one more day. But I do need it tomorrow."

"Yeah, yeah, I got you," Trace said, turning to leave again. "I love you!" he called over his shoulder before he disappeared out of his mother's sight.

He took a long, hot shower, and when he got out and wiped the moisture off the mirror, he took a closer look at his face. Already, the bruise was starting to yellow, the signs of healing. He was glad. When he showed up at school tomorrow, he would hardly even have a bruise, and no one would be able to think that Carter McDuffie beat him up too badly.

After he changed into a clean pair of pants and a simple T-shirt that he would throw a hoodie over when he left again later, he flopped down on his butt and turned on his TV. He wanted to sleep, but he didn't want to deal with another Rezin incident so soon. He also had homework he could work on, but he was too distracted by his thoughts of the day, the fight, his mother, the Albus realm, and Amberly, and he knew he wouldn't be able to get anything done. Productivity wasn't possible when he felt like this.

He waited until the others texted in the group chat that their family was asleep and they were ready to sneak out and go to The White Forest. Then he grabbed his Pentfire. He pulled on his hoodie. He left his room and saw his mom passed out, yet again, on the sofa. Knowing she wouldn't wake up from it, he kissed her softly on the forehead before he snuck out of his house and was greeted by the orange sky.

The walk to The White Forest didn't take long, but it was hard to figure out where the others were waiting since they all had to remain hidden and out of sight from firefighters. Already, being this close to the edge of the dense brush, even though where they met up hadn't been burned by the fire yet, the smoke was heavier, and Trace began to cough.

"Over here!" a voice whisper-yelled. Trace looked to his right and saw a hand waving from behind a bush. He ran toward it, hunched over, trying to look more like an animal in case anyone saw his outline, and then he ducked down behind the bush and found himself the last to arrive in the group.

Amberly was there, too. She looked like a snowy fox in all-white, her sweater fuzzy and begging for Trace to feel its softness.

She wore that on purpose, he thought. She wanted him to see what he was missing. And he missed it, all right. But what could he do? Their relationship didn't work. *They* didn't work.

"All right, now that we're all here," Kaos started, all of them still ducked behind the bush, trying not to cough. "Rose, do you think you'll still be able to manipulate plants to shoot out of the ground and stuff, even if we walk through charred parts of the forest?"

"I... I think so," she replied. She blended in a lot more with their surroundings than Amberly, wearing a dark green turtleneck and black jeans.

"And Amberly—" Kaos paused and looked her up and down. "Do you think you could have worn something that stood out any *more*?"

Amberly shrugged. "What? When we get to the Albus realm, I want the townspeople to know that I am their guardian angel; come to save them all."

Kire snorted. "It's not like we're saving them anymore. We destroyed a lot of their homes while trying to fight Yash's minions off."

"Yeah," Rose joined in. "Do you think your outfit is even going to still be white by the time we get there?"

Amberly crossed her arms and looked away. "What were you *actually* going to say to me, Kaos?"

"Anyway—Amberly, do you know if you can manipulate the flames to move out of our way?" Kaos asked.

"If I can move water, I'm sure I can move fire," she said.

Kaos rubbed his hands together. "Excellent. And I'll be able to tell if I can hear a firefighter's thoughts nearby. Trace, use your sword if we are attacked by any wild beasts or Rezin, and then use the flames to light the way once we're in the cave. But try not to light anything else on fire, got it?"

"Obviously," Trace snapped. He was still a little bitter about losing the fight that Kaos set up for him without telling him.

Kaos ignored the tone. "Kire, I guess you just let us know if Halo gives you any warnings or ominous messages. And be prepared to pull the shield out if we get trapped in new rings of fire."

"Yep," Kire said.

"Are we ready then?" Trace asked. He was uncomfortable being in the same place as Amberly and wanted to just get this over with.

"Just remember to work as a team," Kire said as a final word of advice. Trace knew it was directed at him. He was passive-aggressively letting him know that he and Amberly needed to put aside their anger at each other for the group's sake. Their abilities need to work well to get them successfully through The White Forest back to the Albus realm's portal.

As they started their journey, passing massive sequoias and stepping over the giant roots in the ground, Rose kept magically bringing up various greenery from the ground, such as trees, bushes, and thick vines. The leaves overhead from the trees that were already there seemed to grow larger and create canopies, blocking out the sky.

"I don't think you need to do that quite yet," Trace told her. "We haven't reached any burned parts."

"Yeah, but the greenery provides oxygen," Rose reminded him. "We want to be able to breathe as easily as possible."

"Good point," Trace said. Until then, he thought Kaos wanted her to grow new plants simply to start the reforestation process after all the destruction his fire had caused.

Rose was in the front of the group since she knew her way around The White Forest better than anyone else.

"It's not looking good," she said after while walking.

"What do you mean?" Kaos asked.

"I thought maybe I could find another route to the cave where we wouldn't have to go through any flames. But it looks like we're going to have no choice."

In the distance, Trace could hear yelling, and he could see the brilliant glow of massive flames eating up all of their surroundings. It was loud, too. Not just the sound of the fire crackling but the helicopters dumping water down. The hoses spraying moisture into the air. The thuds of tree branches and tree trunks falling to the forest floor, unable to any longer support their own weight.

Just to their left, as they wearily neared the flames, a tree splintered and cracked so loudly that they all jumped. Trace was confused as to why this was happening until he noticed the flames at the very top of the tree.

They were in the middle of it now.

"I think it's best if we maybe start running," Kire suggested in a slightly high-pitched voice. The tree began to fall, and as the others ran for it, Amberly used her gauntlet to move the massive thing out of the way. It thudded so loudly to the ground by them that Trace thought there was no way it didn't draw attention to them from the firefighters.

"Coming from the west!" one of the voices yelled.

"They heard that tree," Kaos said, his crown on his head. "They're coming to check the area. We need to go."

The gang resumed sprinting. Then, one of the firefighters appeared around a tree, so they all dropped to the ground on their stomachs; Rose quickly growing vines to cover them all up. And when the coast was clear again, she removed them, and coughing and sputtering, they continued running.

"How much longer?" Amberly asked, creating a pathway through the thick flames with her gauntlet while Rose was unable to grow plants fast enough before they were already destroyed by the fire. It was getting harder to breathe. And it was hot. Trace was drenched in sweat.

"We're getting closer," Rose said, sounding out of breath. Trace knew she was weakening.

"You can do it, Rose," Kire said.

"We are all counting on you," Kaos added.

"Hello?" Amberly called from behind everyone, and she continued to manipulate the flame. "I'm the one keeping us from getting burned alive!"

"Thank you," Trace found himself saying. Amberly turned her head as if she hadn't heard him.

"There!" Kire yelled, pointing straight ahead. Finally, they could see the mouth of the cave.

There was another loud boom directly above their heads, and

Amberly was so busy trying to keep the flames away that she couldn't use her powers to move the next massive tree trunk, which was the width of a small bus, as it started tumbling over them. They were all going to be crushed by it, no matter how fast they ran.

Tracy yelled, looking up at the great weight of the tree that was going to be his cause of death, and just as it was about to land on top of him, he ducked and covered his head with his hands, as if that would help.

But then, no death came. No pain came, either. In fact, nothing had even touched him.

He looked up. The tree was floating above them, as if frozen in mid-air.

Trace looked wildly around. Amberly was still focused on the flames.

But then he saw Halo opened up on the ground. She had opened up a shield big enough to protect all of them, the tree resting on top of the perfect dome she had created.

"Thank you, Halo!" Rose cried. Trace wasn't sure the book could actually hear her, but he said a silent thank you himself.

Since the fire couldn't penetrate the bubble shield, Amberly focused her attention on the tree trunk and moved it out of their way. When it was clear, Kire picked Halo up and closed the book, and the shield disappeared. "Holding that tree up probably took so much of her charge," he muttered as they hurried inside the mouth of the cave, away from the flames.

Trace had never been so glad to be somewhere so dark and damp.

"There are so many caves in this forest," Trace said, panting, his hands on his hips. "How do you know this is the right one?" He was asking Rose, who had led them in here.

"Trust me when I say I really have spent a *lot* of time in this forest."

"Yeah, but not when it's on fire."

"*Trust* me." Rose was panting, too, her hands on her knees and her face pale. "This is the right one."

Trace was a bit concerned that she already seemed so weak when they hadn't even reached the Albus realm to use their powers to clean up after themselves yet. He tried to tell himself that he was part of the team, even with Amberly on it, to see if that would maybe help things.

"Well, buddy," Kaos said, slapping Trace on the back. "Rose says we're in the right place, and I believe her. So why don't you light that sword and lead the way?"

Irritably, Trace followed Kaos's instructions, and they all walked in silence, catching their breath and calming down from their dangerous journey. The cave started to look more and more familiar the deeper they went, and eventually, Trace even recognized the spot where Amberly used a bunch of boulders to keep the entrance to the empty lake where the portal sat at the bottom, hidden. Amberly groaned when she saw all the rocks, like she forgot she was going to have to do more work, and began moving them out of the way again with her gauntlet. Then, finally, there was an opening big enough for them to fit through, and once they got inside, there the portal sat, at the bottom of the drained lake, the marble arch glowing blue and inviting them to enter.

12

The sky in the Albus realm was blue, just like the Earth realm. But it was a different sort of blue. A brilliant blue. A shade like Trace had never seen before. They hadn't been able to see the sky on all of their other trips to the Albus realm because of all the smoke in the air from their battles and the towns getting destroyed. But now, even though it was the middle of the night back in the Earth realm, it seemed to be bright and early in the morning in this realm. Birds chirped—maybe a magical kind of bird—and flowers bloomed. The inclined land they were on allowed Trace to see so much of their surroundings from the field where the portal was hidden. High, thriving corn stalks of colorful corn. Rolling hills of a strange, greenish-purple hue. The tall black mountain with the sharp, jagged cliffs and old, crumbling castle. Large bodies of water shimmering in the sunlight. Dense wooded areas, some of the leaves on the trees an oddly vibrant pink color.

"It looks so different," Rose breathed, coming to stand beside Trace.

"It's incredible," he said.

"Well, from here, it looks it," Kire joined in. "But we have a lot of work to do."

"Something tells me you're *excited* about cleaning and fixing and building and basically spending an entire day or more doing chores," Trace pointed out to him.

Kire shrugged. "I like using my hands."

Trace rolled his eyes and looked behind him. Amberly and Kaos were together in their own little corner, talking in hushed tones to each other, saying things that Trace couldn't hear.

"Aye," he said, bothered by what he saw, "why don't we all *come together* and figure out where we're going to go first?"

"Amberly is not feeling well," Kaos said, speaking for her. It was strange because Amberly loved to talk. It could only have meant that what Kaos said was true.

"I'm not feeling so hot, either," Rose admitted, giving Kire a faint smile.

"You two put a lot of work in for us to get here safely," Kire said. "You need some rest and nourishment."

"I'll cut down some corn," Trace offered, pulling out his Pent-fire, eager to put it to use.

"I can get my own corn," Amberly piped up.

"Just listen to what your body needs, and rest, Amberly," Trace instructed, fighting back the eye roll.

He waited—and was fully anticipating—for her to snap back and keep arguing with him, but again, to his surprise, she obeyed him and took a seat on a large, smooth boulder. Since it was big enough for two, Rose walked over and joined her.

Trace grew slightly worried. How much of her powers did it take to move all those flames aside and lift that tree off Halo's shield? Especially since their powers weren't working to the best of their abilities. Trace knew it to be true because the flames on his sword were still weak.

They didn't have to worry about time passing in the Earth realm because they had quickly come to the realization that what was hours or days here was only mere minutes once they were back on Earth. But the strange thing, which Kaos pointed out, was that once they were *back* in the Earth realm, it seemed as if time moved in unison again with the Albus realm, for when they returned to the Albus realm, it was clear much more time had passed from when they last entered it.

"It's not like we're simply on another planet or in another country," Kaos had said with a shrug when they tried to do the math and figure out how it was possible. "This is another realm. It has a whole other set of rules. Physics and gravity and nature even have a whole new set of rules."

Trace started a small campfire, Kire cooked the corn, and Kaos fetched the girls some water from the creek. After a couple hours, when they had gained their energy back, they were ready to get started.

"Where to first, then?" Trace asked, eager to have something to do other than stand around, trying not to memorize every detail of Amberly's face so that he could think about her later.

Kire pulled the teleportation rock out of his backpack. "I say we head to one of the villages and start clearing away rubble."

"Don't forget," Kaos pointed out, "we still need to go find Albus's house."

"But we have no idea where it is," Kire reminded him. "So we will need to ask somebody for directions."

Refusing to admit that Kire was right, Kaos simply tightened his jaw and touched his hand to the stone. "What are we waiting for then?" he asked the others. They all joined in, and just as he had been when he stepped through the portal, Trace felt the world fall away from under his feet. As his stomach rolled, he hardly had time to process where he was and what was happening before he was suddenly standing again somewhere completely new.

He remembered this town. It was the very first one they had stepped foot in after their long journey when they first came to the Albus realm. He could tell it used to be a quaint, artful little village with the Tudor buildings and dirt and cobblestone-lined streets, but it also seemed as if it was a poorer village because everything had crumbled so easily. Structures didn't have the best crafts-manship.

It was a lot different from the last time they had been there as well. Mainly because there were *actual* villagers walking about. The last time they were in the Albus realm, they hadn't met a single person who lived there other than two Albuses, Gertrude and the strange prophet. All of the villages had been deserted, and Trace feared that everyone had died but hoped that they were all just in hiding.

These people were very curiously dressed in colorful garments that did not match their sullen expressions. And as the quintets entered the square, they got a lot of strange looks.

"I bet we look really odd showing up dressed like this," Rose commented in a whisper.

"Glad you can finally see it," Amberly teased.

"I wouldn't exactly say *we're* the ones dressed weird," Trace said, staring at the nearest villager who was digging around some rubble, humming a sad tune. His colorful garments looked like something Trace would wear if it was wacky pajama day at school… in the 1800s. Bright robes. Fluffy collars. Funny slippers.

"Being in *their* world, we are," Rose argued.

"We're drawing attention to ourselves," Kire said.

"I also highly doubt they walk around with flaming sword and crowns on their heads," Amberly added.

"Who are you?"

The voice was so near and so sudden that all five of them jumped. A man had appeared, dressed far less colorfully than all of the others. He had grayish skin, too. Dark black hair and black eyes. He looked as if he never had fun a day in his life.

"Um, hello," Kire said awkwardly. "We've come to help."

"Help?" He had an accent. And it was thick. If they lived in the Earth Realm, Trace would have guessed they lived somewhere in Europe.

"We've been battling and destroying the creatures who ruined your village," Kire continued. "And we think that the battle is over now, so we'd like to help rebuild."

"A bunch of children?" another man asked, approaching. He looked much more colorful than the gray one. He still had the same thick accent. He looked gloomy, but not as much so as the gray man.

"We don't trust strangers here," the gray man said. As the two addressed them, more people started to gather, wanting to watch the scene, curious as to who these kids were. "I am an officer here," he added. "And I've got plenty of torture chambers in our prison."

"We mean no harm, truly," Rose said in a squeaky voice. "We were given gifts, you see. To help fight. And protect. We've been getting help from Albus."

"From Albus?" the colorful man asked. "Which Albus?"

"Uh…" The gang looked at each other.

"Albus Bridge?" Rose tried.

The men were confused. "They're *all* Albus Bridge," the gray one said.

"Um… he is old? Long white hair and beard?" Trace added.

"Quit fooling around, boy," the gray man scolded, putting a hand on his sword in its sheath.

"I think they really don't know," a nearby woman in a bright yellow gown with matching slippers said. "All Albuses have white hair and beards."

"He's married to Gertrude," Trace tried, scanning the crowd, waiting for someone to tell him that they were all married to Gertrudes as well.

"Oh, *Gertrude*'s Albus," the gray man said.

"Well, if they know Gertrude, then I highly doubt they're lying," the colorful man responded.

"They're from another realm," a groggy, old-sounding voice said from somewhere in the crowd. People parted to see who was talking, and it revealed a small old man with a cane. While he was dressed in vibrant purple and looked to be the same age as Albus,

Trace could tell he wasn't as magical as him. Something about him looked so... average. "The Earth realm. A long time ago, when I was very young, we used to be able to move between the two realms. They are telling the truth. See what they're wearing? They've been given the ultimate gifts to provide their realm and ours with protection."

Kaos climbed on top of a particularly large piece of building that had crumbled so that everyone in the crowd—which was very large now, filled with mostly men, but some women and children as well—could see him. "The man is right," he said, his hands on his hips as he puffed his chest out. "Your realm was attacked, and we sent those beasts away. Without us, your entire world would likely have been destroyed."

Kire climbed up as well to join him, laughing nervously. "Uh, that sounded really cocky," he said apologetically. "We're just here to help. It's as simple as that."

Kaos glowered at him and looked like he wanted to push him off the wall.

The crowd began talking at once. "I don't know if we should trust them," someone called.

"They're just kids, helpless kids," another one said.

"What's Albus doing giving magical gifts to a bunch of teenagers?"

"And for God's sake, *what* are they wearing?"

Amberly also joined them on the piece of wall. She didn't say a word to anyone. Instead, she used her gauntlet to pick up another wall that had toppled over behind the crowd. She lifted it upright and then used other pieces of material to keep it from falling back down.

Rose quickly joined in, manipulating plants to hold the structure together.

Everyone was wordless as they watched the two work in perfect unison. Together, Amberly and Rose practically rebuilt an entire house.

By the end of it, Trace was certain they had finally won the townspeople's approval. He was the last one to remain on the ground, so he climbed up the wall and joined the others.

"So, what do you guys say?" he asked, addressing the crowd. "Are you satisfied?"

The crowd cheered and clapped.

"Thank you, thank you," Kaos said after a while of soaking it all up. The teenagers smiled at each other. Trace even caught Amberly's eye, and she was smiling, too. But when she realized she was smiling at Trace, she quickly looked away.

"Also," Kaos asked. "We need directions to Gertrude's Albus's home. Can anyone tell us where we might find it?"

"I can," the colorful man they first spoke to said, stepping forward. Kire hopped off the wall and pulled Halo out of his bag. Using his magical quill, he opened to a blank page. "Could you explain it to me?" he asked.

"You're going to write directions in that?" Amberly asked, scratching her nose.

"Halo will be able to recite them and keep us on the right path," he told her with a side-eye.

"That's genius," Rose said, beaming at him. Trace watched the two smile at each other, thinking he wouldn't be surprised if Rose hopped off the wall to plant a kiss on his lips right in front of everyone.

Gross.

While the man gave Kire instructions to Albus's home, the rest of the group got started on helping the townspeople rebuild. Trace used his own strength to move things around and lift heavy material.

"This place was so deserted before," he said to a guy he was helping carry a long piece of lumber. "Where did everyone go? When the attack happened?"

"A lot of us fled," he said. He looked to be only a little bit older than Trace. But he had an equal amount of muscles. "A lot of us also died. The ones who couldn't make it out in time. But over in the hills, it's a good place to hide."

"I'm sorry for your loss," Trace said, hanging his head slightly as they dropped the lumber to the ground by the house they were working to rebuild.

"I reckon we would have lost a lot more if you guys hadn't shown up," he said. Then, to Trace's surprise, he even offered him a bit of a smile.

It only confirmed how much Trace liked it here. He felt he was somewhere he belonged. Somewhere, he was important. Somewhere where he made a real difference. Part of him, in the wildest bits of his imagination, wished he could stay here forever.

AFTER DOING a good amount of cleaning and repairing and after taking another long break so that the hardest workers, Amberly and Rose, were able to get a good rest, they decided it was time to start their journey to Albus's house, following the directions that Kire had taken down inside of Halo. He had been right about Halo reciting the correct way for them to go. As they walked, after saying goodbye to everybody, any time they made a wrong turn or got slightly confused, Halo was there to write out to Kire how to get them back on track.

"I wish we could just take the rock," Trace eventually grumbled. "I'm sick of walking."

"Well, once we've been there before, we will be able to use the rock afterward," Kire reminded him.

"That doesn't help me now, though."

"Quit your whining," Kaos said, shaking his head.

Don't even get any thought started, Trace thought about his "best" friend. He was still mad about the fight Kaos made him partake in without even telling him about it ahead of time. Thanks to him, the entire school thought he was some sort of weakling. And sure, maybe Kaos didn't know that Carter McDuffie was going to turn out to be Rezin. Still, Kaos was the one who prepared the fight.

The more they walked, the more the group got slightly separated from one another, splitting off, Kaos and Amberly walking much further ahead in the group than the other three.

"It's weird to not see you up there with them," Kire pointed out to Trace.

"Yeah, no duh," Trace replied.

"Does it bother you?" Rose asked.

Trace shot her a dirty look. "I don't care. It's whatever." But of course it bothered him. Kaos was *his* friend. Not Amberly's. Maybe Kaos was just trying to be nice since Amberly didn't get along with anyone else in the group. Still, Kire was Amberly's *brother*. Why couldn't *they* just hang out or something?

"I actually wanted to talk to you about that," Kire said, sounding slightly uneasy. Trace was walking in the middle of Rose and Kire, which he also felt was odd. Usually, especially lately, Kire and Rose couldn't stay away from each other. It was rare that Trace didn't see them holding hands or draping their arms around each other ever since their most recent battle inside of the Albus realm.

"What?" Trace asked in a flat voice. They were far enough away from the other two that they could have this conversation without worrying about them overhearing. Still, Trace was uneasy about it as well.

"Something weird kind of happened," Kire started. He cleared his throat, and Trace sensed he felt awkward about whatever it was he was about to say. "Amberly sort of... came to me after you two broke up."

Trace nearly stopped walking. "She *came* to you?" What the heck did that mean?

Kire nodded. "Yeah. I know, super weird. She's really upset about the breakup. I know she doesn't exactly look like it, and she doesn't do a good job showing it but just know that the way she behaves in front of you is a complete and total act. She's secretly a mess, Trace."

Trace looked up at Amberly's back while she walked next to Kaos. When she turned her head to the side, and he caught sight of her profile, she was laughing at something Kaos was saying. She certainly didn't look too upset.

"I call bull," he decided to say to Kire.

"I..." Kire noticed the way Amberly was laughing as well. "I get it. That looks bad. But, you should've seen her, Trace. I mean... she talked to *me*. Me about *you*. That right there has to tell you all you need to know about it."

"I have to agree with Kire," Rose chimed in.

"Of course you have to agree with him. He's your boyfriend," Trace said.

"Even if he wasn't, I still would. I may have some negative feelings toward Amberly, but I feel like you two being together made her a better person. With you broken up, I'm worried about how nasty she's going to get."

"She doesn't even seem like she feels like being that mean, though," Kire told her. "She walks around the school like a zombie and is always so quiet now."

"Yeah... but this is just because she's grieving. Once she gets past that stage and moves onto just being angry about it... *phew*. It is not going to be pretty."

"You two honestly think that I shouldn't have broken up with her?" Trace asked. "Even after everything you saw between us? Come on. We weren't getting along. She never wanted to be around me. Everything I said and did made her mad. You don't even know how many times I was pathetic around Kaos, trying to get his advice so that I could figure out how to help Amberly and make her feel better after her mom died. His advice ended up being crap."

"I could've told you that," Rose said. "I didn't know that he had been advising you. Because it seems like you sort of pushed yourself away from her, Trace. And she probably really needed you."

"Yeah. Kaos advised it. He said that Amberly really wanted space."

"What does Kaos know?" Kire asked, shooting a dirty look at the back of Kaos's head. "He's never had a girlfriend."

"He could if he wanted to," Trace said, unsure why he was defending him. Kaos was a popular guy. And sure, some people thought it was strange how he sometimes wore his crown to school and that he always wore black, but he had tons of money for one, and he was also not that bad-looking.

"Do you think maybe you and Amberly should talk?" Kire asked. "If you guys can sort things out, I know it would be really good for the group, and—"

Trace interrupted him. "I'm not talking to her, Kire." He stopped walking. "You're seriously taking her side?"

"I'm not taking anyone's side," Kire replied as he and Rose stopped walking with him. "It's just a suggestion."

"How can you even want to be with Rose after the stunt she pulled?" He asked Kire.

"What stunt?"

"Trying to sacrifice herself for the portal. Don't you think it clearly means she doesn't care enough about you if she was so willing to just leave you behind like that?"

"That's not true!" Rose gasped.

Kire's eyebrows wrinkled. "I don't think that at all, actually," he told Trace. "She wasn't trying to get at me by sacrificing herself. It wasn't about me. It was about something so much bigger."

Trace had a very hard time seeing it any other way. He felt betrayed and abandoned by Amberly. Getting worked up, he decided it was better to keep his mouth shut.

"You guys just need to work on your communication. You shouldn't have broken up. You should have worked through your issues. It feels like you just gave up," Rose said.

"You know what?" Trace growled. "I don't need this. Leave me alone."

He resumed walking, speeding up in the direction of Kaos and Amberly but not reaching them entirely. Kire and Rose seemed able to sense that he no longer wanted to walk beside them, and they lingered behind, the quintets walking in three separate groups. They were not united at all.

Thankfully, the route to Albus's home took them to the outskirts of a lot of the other towns and villages that still had so much damage done to them. They didn't have time to stop and help every single one of them. They would eventually resume helping with reparations, but now, getting to Albus's wife was most important. And, just the way they were, staying on the outskirts of all of the villages was for the best so that they weren't stopped and questioned like they had been back in the first village.

They eventually came to a very steep hill, where the clouds sat incredibly low in the sky. The further they walked up this hill, a couple of them huffing and puffing from the strenuous workout, they actually reached the clouds and walked *through* them.

"I always wondered what clouds felt like," Rose said mistily, reaching her hands out to feel the air. Clouds didn't really feel like anything. It just felt especially humid and hard to see.

"How much longer?" Kaos asked over his shoulder at Kire, who was at the end of the group reading his Halo book.

"Shouldn't be far," he called.

"Thank God," Amberly and Rose said at the same time. Then,

despite their dislike for each other, they both giggled a little bit. Rose was out of breath, and Amberly had complained a little bit ago that her feet were killing her. Trace was exhausted, too. They might as well have been climbing a ladder; that's how steep this hill was.

Then suddenly, when Trace was about to say they needed to take a break even though they couldn't see five feet in front of them, which was risky, they broke through the clouds. They were so high up in the sky that it looked like it was nighttime. It wasn't at all how it would have looked if they were back on Earth. That steep incline walk wouldn't have taken them to the edge of the atmosphere. The distance between the ground and the sky in the Albus realm was much, much shorter than in the Earth realm.

But at the edge of the hill, there was only one thing awaiting them. A magnificent, gigantic, vibrantly lit tree.

They could see nothing beyond it, for the hill sloped back downward, and covering it was a thick layer of clouds. This realm's moon shined brilliantly, backlighting a tree. The stars twinkled brighter than any Trace had ever seen back in his realm. And the tree was lit up because of all of the windows carved into its mansion-sized trunk. Albus's home was inside of it.

The windows were of various shapes and sizes. Some had clear panes. Others had stained glass. The light cascading out of the house was warm and yellow, a stark contrast against the brilliant white of the stars twinkling behind it.

There was a small front gate made of wood that surrounded the entirety of the trunk, and in the little yard, there was a lush garden, the plants all aligned in the order of the colors of the rainbow. There were fruits and vegetables growing that Trace had never seen before. But they were so bright and luscious that he was eager to try them. And it *had* been a while since he last ate. The town they helped rebuild had fewer means than others, which meant it didn't have as appealing-looking food.

His stomach growled.

"Think we can eat some of that?" he asked the others.

They approached the gate, all of them standing by each other for the first time the entire walk.

"I can't believe you can even think about food right now," Rose said, shaking her head.

Before they could even open the wooden gate and make their walk up the path to the stained glass front door, it opened wide in front of their very eyes.

A tall, very thin, very old woman with long white hair piled high on her head exited the house and started down the path right in their direction. She moved like she floated, which Trace hadn't been expecting for somebody who looked so weak. But he knew Gertrude couldn't be a normal woman. Not if she had been married to Albus.

The sight of her reminded Trace why they were here, and instantly, the food was forgotten. Instead, his growling stomach twisted into knots.

"Gertrude," Kaos said, sounding rather businesslike. He was never great at showing sympathy or sadness. But Trace was glad he was taking charge and doing the talking. He had no clue how to break the news of her husband's death—which was their fault— to her.

Already, when Gertrude reached them, her luminescent pink eyes were full of great sadness. "I was wondering when you five would arrive," she told them in a shaky voice. Gertrude was wearing a long silk robe, the color of the dark sky outside. And also like the sky, it was dotted with white, like stars in a galaxy. Her nose was long and narrow, as Albus's had been, and her skin was wrinkled and pale. She had thin lips surrounded by smile lines. It was as if Albus used to make her smile very, very often.

"I am sorry to say that we have some not-good news," Kaos told her, still on the other side of the gate with the others.

"I already know," she said, nodding her head slowly and

solemnly. "I knew of my husband's passing the instant it happened. I felt it deep inside my soul."

"I'm so sorry," Amberly told the woman, surprising Trace. And as he looked at the others, he saw the shock on their faces, too. Quickly, Amberly began shaking with her sobs. And Gertrude opened the wooden gate to console her. She wrapped her arms around Amberly, and Amberly cried into her robe. The others stood there, not knowing what else to do.

"Shush, dear girl," Gertrude said to Amberly, patting her back as she held her. Then she guided her in the direction of the whimsical house, nodding with her head for the others to follow. As she led the way, she whispered things to Amberly that no one else could hear, and by the time they walked through the front door, Amberly had calmed down quite a bit. But Trace could see that the others still looked deeply upset. Rose had silent tears cascading down her cheeks, and Kire's eyes were a bit bloodshot. Kaos looked sad, but he didn't look anywhere near tears. Trace felt more sick to his stomach than anything. Albus being dead. Amberly breaking down like that. It was almost more than he could take.

"You guys must be tired from your long journey," Gertrude said. She took a seat on a small wooden chair at a small wooden table that sat at the base of a winding staircase. Everything inside of the house had a slight curve to it to match the shape of the tree trunk. And everything was made of a pinkish-yellow wood. It was as if the stairs and walls and much of the furniture were carved right out of the trunk itself. There were lots of candles lit and a roaring fireplace, and Trace thought vaguely how unsafe it seemed.

"We're fine," Kaos said, speaking for everyone and not speaking honestly.

"Nonsense," Gertrude said. "Please sit."

There were plenty of options to choose from. Tree trunk stools. Plush cushions on top of wooden carved sofas, the legs of them built right into the ground. More wooden chairs around the small table which Gertrude sat at.

Trace opted for one of the stools over by the door. Amberly sat at a chair near the woman as if the two were old friends. Rose and Kire sat on one of the sofas. Kaos remained standing.

"We're all so sorry," Trace said to her, too. "We never meant for Albus to die."

Again, she nodded very slowly. "Of course not. But my husband believes in you five so much that he was willing to do anything to make sure you were successful."

"Why believe in *us*, though?" Kire asked. "We're just a bunch of kids."

"A bunch of kids who have done better at protecting the Earth realm than all of the others who have tried. You must not forget how far you have come," she reminded them.

They were all silent for a beat.

"Your house is just incredible," Rose eventually piped up.

While Gertrude didn't smile, she did look at Rose fondly. "Albus and our son built this home. It took them many, many seasons to do it, and I'll admit I could not for the life of me see their vision. Not until it was finished, and they surprised me with it."

"We shouldn't take up too much of your time," Kaos said. "We just wanted to fill you in on what happened. We should tell you how he died and where his body lies—we buried him together and had a ceremony for it."

"You need not regale that sad tale to me," Gertrude said, "for I already know everything that happened that day."

"You do?" Amberly asked. Everyone looked around at one another.

"How?" Trace asked.

"Because of me."

It was a new voice that spoke. A male one. Harsh sounding. Baritone. It nearly vibrated the house. When Trace looked in the direction of it, he saw a man appear at the bottom of the stairs. And the man was very familiar. Not only because he looked a lot like Albus but because Trace had actually met him before.

"Albus," Trace said when the others just stared at him in shock. This was the man who had been with *their* Albus and Gertrude back in the castle when they had brought Rose and Kire to reunite with Trace, Kaos, and Amberly. It was when they first found out that Albus was still alive after the great war started in their realm. He and Gertrude, and this Albus before them, had all been so weak and tired from all of the fighting.

"Hello again," the man said. His eyes had no pupils and no irises. They were just purely white like Albus's had been. His hair was also long and white. His main difference from their Albus was that his facial features were sharper and gave him a far more intimidating look.

"Oh, I remember you," Rose said, getting to her feet. "You were with Albus and Gertrude in that magical carriage when you found me and Kire a short while back."

"Indeed, young Rose."

Trace wondered what this Albus was doing at Gertrude's house.

"How did you know about what happened to Albus?" Kire asked.

"All Albuses are connected. In a way that is complex and too difficult to begin to explain."

"So you were able to keep Gertrude filled in when Albus came to us on that battlefield," Kaos said.

"Indeed. We all suffered a very great loss that day."

"Do you live here?" Trace blurted out. He realized quickly it wasn't the most important question; he just found that he was curious about it.

"I do not," Albus said. "I am a very good friend of Gertrude and Albus."

"He and my Albus grew up together," Gertrude informed them. "He's like a brother. He's been staying with me to help with all of my husband's affairs."

"We never meant for Albus to sacrifice himself," Rose said. She hung her head. Kire grabbed her hand and held it.

"Of course you didn't," the other Albus replied. He stroked his long beard, which wasn't quite as long as their Albus's and stood beside Gertrude, placing a hand on her shoulder. "Ultimately, he made that decision to place his life in front of all of yours. I know it may seem difficult, but you mustn't blame yourselves."

"This Albus and I do not blame you," Gertrude added.

Trace felt relief. He had been worried when they got here that Gertrude was going to do nothing but yell at them and demand they all pay for the death of her husband.

"There's going to be another ceremony," Gertrude continued. "We are arranging it now. And we'd love for you all to be there. We know where you buried my dear husband, but he belongs at rest with the rest of the Albuses at the great cemetery at the Lake of Wisdom."

"We will be there," Trace said, speaking for everyone without even checking with them first. He didn't need to check with them. He knew they would agree. Even Amberly. At least when it came to Albus, this was the one thing they could all be united about.

The gang hung around Gertrude's home and stayed for a cup of tea and made small talk, and then the teens decided it was probably time for them to move on.

"Thank you so much for having us," Rose said to Gertrude as they all gathered by the door.

Gertrude opened it for them. "Even though I already knew what happened to my husband, I am grateful that you all came to see me."

"Before you go," the other Albus said, still seated in a chair at the table. He looked as if he were simply too tired to stand with the others. Maybe there had been something *besides* tea in his cup. "I want to inform you that when it comes to Albuses, there is a lot we know about one another. Even things we don't want to know. Because of this connection between all of us. We've all shared triumphs and terrors. We've all known love and death. We can feel each other's emotions. It affects our own. But none of that is what I want you to know more than what I have to say next. I know that you have another one of Yash's minions stuck to your realm. Rezin is chained to Earth. And you must beat him."

"We've been working on it," Kaos said.

Albus nodded. "Let this be of help. Albus left behind something that will give you insight. You must find it. That is all I can say about it."

14

The next day, when Trace got in Kaos's car and they made their way to pick up the others before school—*all* of the others—he quickly realized he wasn't the only one still feeling a bit sick from all of the smoke of the fire in The White Forest. It had been quite another ordeal to get out of the forest last night after their visit to the Albus realm, and by the time they made it to safety, they had all been coughing and wheezing, their eyes and lungs burning.

"I just kept thinking about the air in the Albus realm," Kire said when they were all together, making the drive to school. "How clean and fresh it was."

"It's like the two realms reversed," Rose said. "It used to be *that* one that was covered in smoke and fire."

"Now it looks like a fairytale land," Amberly chimed in. She seemed to be in a better mood than usual. Seeing it made Trace smile a little, even though it wasn't as if she was talking to him. He was just glad she had accepted a ride from Kaos at all.

"I'd totally live there," Trace said, voicing what he had thought about yesterday. "Why don't we?"

"Because we are defenders of the *Earth* realm, not the Albus realm," Kaos said. "Our lives and our homes are here."

Trace rolled his eyes, and Kire smirked at him.

"What the—?"

When Trace looked up at Kaos, he saw his friend staring in the rearview mirror. Trace looked over his shoulder and saw a police cruiser behind them, their lights on. They were getting pulled over.

"Were you speeding?" Amberly asked, noticing it, too.

"I don't—I don't *think* so," Kaos said. He didn't have his crown on, or he probably would've easily been able to tell why they were in trouble.

"Well, don't keep driving!" Rose said, her voice shrill. "Pull over!"

"Right." Kaos followed Rose's order and steered his shiny red car to the side of the road. They were right in the middle of the countryside, a vast expanse of land right before they got to the road that led to their school.

Trace watched out the back window as the police officer pulled over behind him and got out of his vehicle. He kept his hand on his belt and walked like he ran this town as he approached Kaos's window. He motioned for him to roll it down, and Kaos obeyed.

The officer peered in at all of them from behind his sunglasses. "You know why I pulled you over today?" the officer asked with a bit of a Southern accent.

"No, sir," Kaos said, a bit of an edge to his voice. As a rebellious teen, it went against everything in his nature to be respectful to a police officer. "I don't have the slightest idea."

"No?" The officer questioned. "You don't know if you were speeding? If you ran a red light? Rolled the stop sign? Forgot your blinker?"

"I don't think I did any of those things," Kaos said. "So, please, why don't you just enlighten me?"

"Kaos," Rose said through her teeth, "be nice."

"Well, the fact of the matter is..." The officer stepped a couple of feet away from the window. Then he looked up and down the completely empty street. "You're driving on a closed road. Notice how there doesn't seem to be anybody else around?"

Trace realized it was a bit strange that no one else had driven past them. This was a pretty common route to school. And, not that he had been paying much attention, but he couldn't remember driving past any closed road signs.

"Closed?" Kaos jeered. "Why is it closed?"

"Oh no," Amberly suddenly said in the seat next to him.

Then the police officer started laughing. But it wasn't a normal laugh. It was a cackle. An evil one.

"No freaking way," Trace breathed. He couldn't believe he didn't see it the second the officer got out of his car. *The dang sunglasses!*

But there was no time for any of them to do anything. They were trapped inside the vehicle, and none of them had their weapons on hand. They all quickly began rummaging around in the car for their gifts, except for Rose, who looked as if she hadn't quite realized what was happening yet.

Rezin, disguised as one of Montgomery's police officers, took a couple more steps back on the empty street. Still laughing, he ripped off his sunglasses and exposed his flaming eyes. Trace's sword was in the trunk, so he was trying to push Kire and Rose out of the way so that he could pull Kaos's back seat forward.

"Stop!" Kire yelled at Trace's pushing because he was trying to dig into his backpack to get Halo out.

Everyone was freaking out. And it got worse when Kaos's car began lifting into the air.

"Guys," Rose cried, looking out the window. "Guys, what's happening?"

"Oh my God!" Amberly gasped as she realized how quickly they were all rising up into the sky. Further and further they went. Rezin had complete control over their vehicle.

"What do we do?" Kaos asked.

"You're the leader!" Amberly screeched.

"Fools!" Rezin yelled from far away, way down below. But even that far away, his voice still had the ability to boom as if it were playing on the radio inside of Kaos's car. "Haven't you learned by now?"

Trace *did* feel like a fool. They should have been on their guard. They should have known Rezin was going to continue to pull stunts like this to catch them by surprise so that he could more easily defeat them.

And this time, it felt like he was finally going to win. None of the quintets had flying abilities. It wasn't like they could just jump out of the car and land safely on the ground. Everything was happening so fast that none had even gotten a hold of their gifts yet to fight back. All Rezin had to do was let go of the car, and they would all die.

"Crap, crap, crap!" Trace yelled, wanting to hit himself. He wanted to hit *all* of them. How hadn't they seen it? Could anyone else see them around town at this high up? Had Rezin blocked off the road to ensure no one *would* see them? Trace was certain Rezin and Yash wanted to keep their magical abilities a secret so that the Earthlings wouldn't begin preparations for a war against aliens. Yash hated when his life was made more difficult. So how was Rezin going to explain a car magically lifting thousands of feet into the sky? How were their deaths going to be explained when their bodies were recovered in the rubble and scrap metal after they were killed by the fall?

The car stopped rising. There was a single moment where Trace felt they were all suspended in the air as if frozen, but then he felt them dropping, his stomach flying to his throat, and his butt lifting out of the seat since he hadn't worn his seatbelt. His back hit the roof of the car, and everyone screamed at the top of their lungs. There was nothing they could do. No way to get out of this. No one had gotten a handle on their gifts in time. Rose had her hand on her Pendantix, but she clearly couldn't focus when she was falling to her death.

Traced closed his eyes and braced himself. His last thoughts were of Amberly and how he still loved her and always would, no matter where his soul carried him. And then suddenly, he felt nothing.

In fact, it was a very *strange* nothing. He felt as if he were standing on his own two feet, like he had teleported out of the car. He didn't feel the pain of death. He didn't feel darkness. In fact, on the other side of his closed eyelids, he was being blinded by a bright light. Was this the tunnel everyone was talking about?

He decided to peek through a slit in his eyelids, wanting to find out.

He was with the others. All of them were on their feet. They were standing in a field.

"What the...?" Trace lost any ability to form any other words because in front of them was a very short human-shaped figure with powder-blue fur and rabbit-like ears.

Dying is weird, he thought.

"H-Halo?" Kire asked the small rabbit creature.

"That's right," the rabbit said. She had an excitable voice and bright, round eyes. "Let me tell you: after *that* save, I'm going to need a *long* time to recharge."

15

"I don't understand," Trace said, completely bewildered and beside himself. "What just happened?"

Kire was still staring, open-mouthed, at Halo. Or at least—that was what Kire was calling the bunny creature.

Slowly looking around, he noticed he wasn't the only one who was completely flabbergasted by what was happening. Had they died? Had the car fallen, and they plummeted to their deaths? Or had Halo really saved them all? And if so, how?

"I didn't know you could pull us *all* in," Kire said.

The rabbit smiled knowingly. Trace had no idea what was happening. But then the rabbit looked at him. He couldn't exactly describe it. But with that one penetrating look, it brought the reality to Trace. This was real. They hadn't died.

"Kire," Rose said slowly, tiptoeing toward her boyfriend and extending her arm out like she wanted to pull him away from the rabbit. "What is this? What's going on?"

"What do you mean by pulling us in?" Amberly added, being the furthest away from everyone, standing by herself. Trace watched the exchange as Kaos turned to her, saw her standing back there alone, and made his way to go and be by her side.

And Trace didn't like it one bit.

"No need to look so afraid of me," Halo the rabbit said. "After all, you should be plenty used to me by now with all of the help I've been giving."

"Oh, guys," Kire said, turning to look at everyone else. He accepted Rose's handhold, and he still looked to be a bit discombobulated. "This is Halo. This is what she looks like."

"A... rabbit..." Kaos trailed off.

Trace turned back to stare at it some more. He supposed he didn't even picture Halo to *have* a figure. He just saw it as a book. And nothing more. A book with a mind.

"What, you've never met a talking rabbit before?" she asked, shrugging and turning away from everyone. She started walking, and everyone looked at each other.

"Are we supposed to follow?" Trace asked in a quiet voice, not wanting the strange creature to hear him.

"That's the idea," the rabbit called over her shoulder.

"This has only happened to me once before," Kire said. "I had no idea *this* could happen."

"Well then..." Rose said after the rabbit. "I guess we should follow her."

"You don't want to get lost in this world of nothingness," Halo called over her shoulder. "Trust me."

Without further ado, the gang grouped up and followed behind Halo. Trace was walking right beside Amberly. But she didn't look at him.

"Where are we going?" Kire asked.

"If you can save us by pulling us into the book, why didn't you do that before?" Kaos asked before the rabbit could answer the first question. "All of those times we were in battles, near death. What if you had just sucked Albus into the book before he killed himself?"

"I was already a great deal weaker by those times," Halo explained, opting to answer Kaos's question instead of Kire's. "You see, I need to charge and recover. Pulling someone into my world is exhausting. Depleting. I cannot do it often. And during that last battle, when Albus did pass, I had already taken up a lot of my energy using a shield to protect you all. There wasn't enough power in me to do that. It is a rare occurrence. One that cannot happen often. So don't get used to this. But, while I have you all here, I might as well show you something."

"Show us what?" Amberly asked.

"You'll see, silly girl with silly shoes."

Trace looked down at Amberly's feet. She was wearing heels. And as they walked through the field, up the hill, he deemed them to be insensible.

"These are expensive," she snapped bitterly.

Halo pretended as if she hadn't heard her.

They were about to reach the top of the hill. What awaited them on the other side of it?

"I figured I could have written this all out to Kire," the rabbit continued. "But it is probably best that I just show you."

Trace was beginning to feel out of breath from the walk. He couldn't believe it. He had just thought he was going to die. And now here he was, in a whole new world.

Finally, they reached the peak of the hill. They all stood in a straight line as they stared down the other side of it.

Fire. Destruction. A town crumbled to nothing.

"What is this?" Trace asked, his voice escaping him and making the words come out in a whisper.

"It's your world," Halo said.

"What are you talking about?" Amberly snapped. "What is this from? The White Forest fire? Does it get bigger or something?"

"Goodness no," Halo replied. "Trust me, a silly forest fire could not create a mess like this."

"Then what could?" Kire asked.

"I think..." Kaos trailed off, and his face twisted into one of fear and confusion.

"What?" Trace asked him.

"If you were thinking that a mess like this could have only been done by Yash, you would be correct." Halo looked regrettable for saying it.

Trace couldn't peel his eyes away from the scene. "Is this the future?" he asked, feeling nauseated. "But... but... we closed the portal. Yash can't get to Earth anymore. Does Rezin do this or something? No. *No.* There's just no way."

"But there *is* a way," Halo said.

"What are you talking about?" Kire bit out, his fingers curling into fists. "Halo, we closed the portal."

This wasn't happening.

"You think the earth no longer needs to be saved, don't you?" Halo asked them.

"Well, seeing as we closed the portal off to him, yes?" Amberly asked. She had nothing but attitude for Halo, in typical Amberly fashion.

"I am sorry to break this news to you, but everything is not what it seems back in your world."

"I don't get it," Kire said. He looked close to tears. "We did everything we were supposed to. Albus... He died, Halo. He risked his life to help us close the portal. Are you telling me that Yash can still get to Earth? That Yash still has a way to destroy it?"

It was unimaginable to hear it. Unimaginable to picture it. They had worked so hard. They had done so much fighting. Yash was supposed to be a thing of the past. They were supposed to only have Rezin to worry about now. They didn't think Rezin was capable of ending the world. They just thought him a nuisance that they needed to figure out how to destroy before he destroyed them.

The tension in the air was high as they all waited for Halo to answer them. She clasped hands together in front of her—or were they called 'paws'?—and bowed her head briefly. Then she looked back up at all of them. "I am afraid there is still a way for Yash to end all of you."

TRACE DIDN'T THINK he would mind if he was never pulled inside the book of Halo ever again. He hated the way it felt. The falling sensation. The squeezing at his stomach and his head. The whooshing noise floating through his ears. The sensation of everything squeezing and then releasing.

And when he was back on his own two feet in the Earth realm, the first thing he saw was that Kaos had arrived before him. And Kaos's back was turned to him as he stared at the mess that was his car. It was a hunk of crushed metal and busted windows, scraps, and glass all around them.

Kaos sank to his knees.

Trace put his hands on his own knees, hunching over in trying to get rid of the dizziness. He felt horrible for Kaos. His car meant everything to him.

"You're telling me, after all of that," Kire said, being the only one to speak as they all stared at Kaos's totaled car, "we still have to go to school?"

"My car," Kaos said.

"Why did Halo make us leave?" Rose asked. "Why would she just tell us such monumental news that Yash can still destroy Earth but then make us leave without even telling us how, when, or why?" Her eyes were glistening. And when Trace glanced at Amberly, he noticed Rose wasn't the only one who wanted to cry.

"Amberly?" Trace asked in a gentle tone.

She averted her gaze and walked over to Kaos instead, kneeling down beside him to comfort him about his destroyed car. Even though this was a common road to take to school, no other vehicles had yet to pass by. Rezin must have created a blockage somehow.

Trace was overwhelmed. He didn't know what they were going to do about Kaos's car. How they were going to explain it to anyone. They had all magically gotten out unscathed. *Literally* magically. No one would buy it. And then there was the Yash situation. The devastating, absolutely crushing news that the earth was still in danger. Just when Trace thought he could rest again, the easiness was stripped from him. The certainty was completely gone. Now, he thought he'd never rest easy again.

MIRACULOUSLY, though Trace thought it had been a nearly impossible task, he made it through the school day. He had to take the bus home for the first time practically since Kaos first got his license—he was gifted the car on his sixteenth birthday.

When he walked in through the front door of his home, his mother was having a coughing fit on the couch.

"Are you all right?" Trace asked immediately, dropping his backpack to the floor and rushing over to her side.

"I..." She could not even finish her sentence because she was coughing so much.

"Mom?"

She held up her hand, and with his body trembling, he waited for her coughing fit to pass. What if it didn't? He had needed to come home first to get the money out of its hiding spot in his room before he could go down to the pharmacy. Originally, he had planned for Kaos to drop the others off first and then wait for him outside so he could grab the money and go to the pharmacy together. But now he had no ride. It was going to take him a bit longer to get it than usual. But he was pretty sure he could dig his bike out of the garage. Hopefully, it had air in the tires. He hadn't used it in forever.

"I'm all right," his mom finally answered. "Do you have my medicine, Trace? I told you I needed it today."

"I'm going to get it right now," he said. "I just... Kaos is busy... So I have to take my bike." He didn't want to explain to her that Kaos's car had been in a wreck. Especially when they hadn't been in it.

The others, Kire, Rose, and Amberly, went with Trace back to school. Kaos stayed behind to deal with the *real* police, his father helping him. Trace still didn't have any idea what Kaos told the officers or his parents about what happened. Kaos just told everyone that he'd figure it out and talk to them later. He never showed up at school. And he still hadn't texted any of them back yet. But, bitterly, Trace almost wondered if maybe Kaos and Amberly were texting, separate from the group chat.

I'm being stupid, he thought to himself. *Why am I getting a jealous feeling about Amberly and Kaos? Like anything would ever happen with them.*

"Your bike," his mom repeated. "You haven't gotten on that thing in forever."

He was about to smile at her, but then she reached for something on the coffee table.

A beer.

"Mom." He snatched it from her hand. "Seriously?"

Normally, Trace was pretty sure he wouldn't say anything to her. That he would just let her drink the beer and waste her life away like she always had. But Trace was getting fed up. With everything. And now, with the worry of Yash still coming down to destroy the earth, he had to think about things like this. What if, when the world was falling apart, his mom was too drunk to even get off the couch? What if he couldn't get her to run? What if he couldn't get her anywhere safe?

She needed to stop this.

"Did you really just take that from me?" she snapped back. She was shocked. But of course she was. Because Trace never acted this way. But he was sick being silent about it.

"Yeah. I did." He got to his feet. "You need to cut this out, Mom,"

"Excuse me?"

"Stop drinking."

"I'll do as I please," she retaliated.

Trace started collecting everything off the coffee table. All of the unopened beers, along with the bottle of wine and the shooters of liquor. "No, you won't. Because doing what you please is going to end up getting you killed. And then what will happen to me? Huh? Did you ever even consider it? Do you ever think about anyone besides yourself?"

She tried to get to her feet but was weak. "Trace, stop!" she yelled, frantic. She grabbed Trace's arms, trying to get some of her alcohol back. It was as if she would die without it.

But she was going to die with it, too.

"Stop, let go!" Trace yelled as she grabbed his arms and didn't let him pull away from her. "You can't have it!"

To his disbelief, his mother was crying now. "You can't just walk in here and control me! You're acting just like your father, Trace!"

"Good!" he yelled out, not meaning it after the words were out. He hated it when she said that. He didn't want to be anything like his father. His mother feared his father. But maybe what Trace needed right now was for his mother to fear him, too. To fear him enough that she wouldn't try to stop him when he threw out all of her alcohol.

His mother froze, dropping her hands from his body. She was frigid. The only thing moving at all was the tear down her cheek. Then, finally, in a low, quiet voice, she said, "You don't mean that."

"You gotta stop, Mom," he said, his voice cracking.

Without letting her get another word in, he left the room with all of the alcohol. He walked outside to the dumpster and tossed all of it. Would she spend the last little money she had to go and buy more, probably right after he left to get her medicine? It was likely. But this felt good for now, at least. It didn't feel good to make his mother cry, of course. It didn't feel good to hurt her feelings. But it felt good to get rid of her alcohol.

Once it was all disposed of, he went back inside the house and into his bedroom to find the cash from his last fight. But wait... where was it?

When he checked his secret hiding spot, in between his mattress and his box spring, in that brown envelope, it was gone.

"Mom!" he yelled. "Were you in my room?"

He got no response from her.

Trace doubted she had been in there anyway. She was too weak to hardly get off the couch, much less walk around his room in search of money. Besides, if she did find money, she would have known that he needed it to buy her medicine.

Or did she care about getting more alcohol more?

He began tearing his room apart. He dug through his closet. He rifled through his bookcase. He got on his hands and knees and searched under his bed. The more time that passed without finding the money, the angrier he got. He started growling. Then yelling. Then kicking and hitting stuff.

"Where is it?!" he yelled.

If his mom could hear him having his tantrum inside his bedroom, she didn't say anything about it.

He didn't understand it. His mom was home all the time. If someone had broken in to take it, she would have known.

"It couldn't have just disappeared into thin—!" He cut himself off when the realization smacked him in the face.

The money disappeared into thin air.

Because Rezin took it.

"You've got to be kidding me!" he yelled, punching the wall so hard his fist went straight through it.

"What was that?" his mom finally called from somewhere in the living room. She was probably still on the couch.

"Don't worry about it!" he snapped. "I-I'll be right back."

His mother needed the medicine. Today. As he left his room to go into the garage, he could hear her starting up another coughing fit. But Trace didn't have the money to get the medicine.

He hopped on his bike—thankfully, it still had air in the tires—and raced down the street to Kaos's house. Once there, he pounded on the door, sweating and coughing from the bad air quality and how hard he had pumped his legs.

"Hey, man," Kaos said when he answered the door.

Trace was a frantic mess. "The money is gone!" he cried out. "Rezin took it. Kaos, I needed that money! My mom could literally die if she doesn't have her medicine!"

He couldn't believe he had been so stupid to leave it unprotected. He should have kept it close to him, in his pocket or in a safe pouch around his neck or something. Now, his mom's life was at risk.

Kaos looked like he had already had a very long day, but Trace did not care to ask him about it. He didn't care to know what happened with the car or his parents or if the police had suspected anything. All he cared about right now was replacing the money that Rezin took.

"Trace, it's all good," Kaos said in a calm voice. "We'll get more money."

"How?" Trace asked. "Are you going to give me some? Steal some from your rich parents?"

"Not from them." There was a twinkle in his eye.

Trace grabbed him by the shirt collar. "This is no time for games!" he shouted.

Kaos stepped away from him. "Trace, chill!"

"Help me!"

Thankfully, Kaos's parents let him borrow one of their cars, a beautiful, sparkling Mercedes, and Kaos sped through the town, pulling into the nearest corner store.

"What are we doing here?" Trace asked, anger still very evident in his tone.

"What's the easiest way for us to get you more money?" Kaos asked him.

Trace just stared at him.

Kaos pulled his backpack from the backseat and took his crown out of it. He placed it on his head. "Just follow my lead."

They went inside the corner store. There were some other customers at the counter and wandering through the snack aisle. So, at first, Trace followed Kaos around as they browsed through the shelves. "We have to wait for them to leave," he whispered to Trace.

That's when Trace realized it. Were they going to rob the place? "Kaos..."

"Don't worry about it."

Of course he was worried about it. They were about to become criminals!

When they were alone in the dingy, dirty corner store with the young man behind the counter, Kaos put his hands in his pockets and casually approached him. The person behind the counter didn't even look old enough to consume alcohol. He was scrawny and pimply with greasy hair.

"If you want some cigarettes, I'm definitely going to need ID, Your *Highness*," the guy said to Kaos, eyeing his crown.

Kaos smiled at him. And then Trace saw the focused look in his eyes. "I'd like for you to give us all of the money in your register."

"Yeah, sure thing," the guy said, immediately obeying him. He opened the cash register and started taking everything out of it.

"And after you give us the money, you're going to destroy the camera footage. And you're not going to remember that you saw us in here."

"You got it."

It felt so wrong. But Trace did nothing to stop it. What else could he do? How else could he get the money to pay for the expensive medication?

Before he knew it, they were outside the corner store, and Trace's pocket was full of cash.

As Kaos drove away, he had a smile on his face. "There. How easy was that?"

"Thank you," Trace told him, finally feeling like he could breathe again.

"Don't mention it."

16

At lunch the next day, the quintets all leaned in close to each other at their table, not wanting their conversation to be overheard by any of their classmates.

"So, can you finally tell us what happened yesterday?" Kire asked Kaos. At first, Trace's stomach dipped. Was he talking about the corner store they robbed?

"It's all taken care of," Kaos said. "I already told you guys."

"But how, exactly?" Kire asked.

Trace felt relieved. But he also felt a little guilty because after they got the money for his mom's medicine yesterday, Kaos took him to the pharmacy to pick it up and then dropped him off at home. Trace was so worked up over everything that had happened yesterday that he completely forgot to check on his friend and make sure everything was okay after his car was destroyed by Rezin.

"When you guys all went to school, I rummaged through the wreckage and got the gauntlet and the sword out of the trunk. Then I hid them away in some bushes and had my dad come. I removed the closed road signs that Rezin set up and just tossed them in the woods. Then, when Dad arrived, I used my powers on him. Made him call the towing company. The towing company arrived. I used my powers on that guy, too. The car is totaled; there's no fixing it. But I made my dad believe that the accident wasn't our fault and that it was a miracle we all got out unharmed. It was easy, really. The gauntlet and the sword are in my locker. Safe and sound."

But Trace wondered if that was entirely true. Because Kaos looked tired today. Maybe all of that manipulation, on top of the manipulation at the corner store, had taken a lot out of him. He was getting good with his powers, but when they weren't all getting along as a team, how much extra effort had it taken to get it to work?

"I'm going to miss that thing," Amberly said, pouting.

"Why aren't you eating?" Trace blurted out, noticing that she didn't even have a tray of food in front of her. He had forgotten that they weren't really talking. It has been instinctual, almost, to just check in on her. Even if she didn't want him to.

She seemed a bit taken aback by the sudden question. "I'm, uh, just not hungry."

"I get what you mean," Rose said, hardly touching her food either. "Because of what Halo told us, right?"

"Yeah."

"Do you think whatever Albus left us that will help defeat Rezin will also help us defeat Yash? Or figure out how to stop him from getting to Earth... again?" Kire asked everyone.

Trace groaned. "This is so annoying. I thought we were done with that. We have to find the thing Albus left us. We have to defeat Rezin. We have to stop Yash *again*. The Albus that is alive won't just tell us where the thing is. And Halo didn't answer a single one of our questions yesterday. Why can't anyone just be upfront?"

"I don't even want to talk about it anymore. At least not right now." Amberly looked pale. "I am still processing it, I think."

"Let's change the subject, then," Trace said, wondering if he sounded like he was trying too hard. It was just that... yesterday, Trace had thought he was about to die. And even then, he was thinking about Amberly. It made it very clear that he still had deep feelings for her. That he didn't want their relationship to be over.

"Okay, did anybody else see the news this morning?" Rose asked.

Everyone stared at her.

"What?" she asked.

"You might be the only teenager on the planet who watches the news in the morning," Amberly said.

Rose rolled her eyes and shrugged. "It was just on when I was eating breakfast. Anyway. You know that little corner store on Fourth Street?"

Oh crap.

"What about it?" Kire asked.

"I used to always swing in there when I had a craving for candy. This guy who had been working there forever, who was always really nice to me when I went in, apparently robbed the place! He robbed his own job! He even tried to destroy the video footage of it. He was apprehended, but he's claiming he has no recollection of taking the money, and he's swearing he doesn't have it. Isn't that weird?"

"What's weird about it?" Kaos asked, looking deeply intrigued and not at all horrified like Trace felt.

"He worked there forever. And just randomly decided yesterday to steal money and then try to claim he doesn't even have the money?"

Trace stared at Kaos. Kaos smiled at him briefly before leaning back and crossing his arms. "Huh. I should have been more thorough with my demands."

"Wait, what do you mean?" Rose asked slowly. Then, her eyes grew with suspicion.

But it was Amberly who figured it out first. "You *robbed* a corner store?!"

"Shush," Trace demanded in a panic. Why did Amberly have to say it so loud?

Amberly lowered her tone and leaned in closer. "Are you *crazy*?"

"Trace, why do you look guilty, too?" Kire asked. "Were you there?"

"I—we—it's a long story," Trace tried.

"What is wrong with you two?" Rose bit out.

"It hadn't been my idea!" Trace defended. He didn't mean to throw Kaos under the bus like that, but even though Kaos had only been helping Trace, Trace himself felt they went about it the wrong way. Like Kaos had used his powers for evil instead of good.

"Do I look like I needed the money?" Kaos asked. "I did it to help a friend. Relax."

"Because of you, some innocent guy is in jail," Rose hissed. "And there's discussion that maybe he had a mental breakdown!"

"I'm sure he'll get through it," Kaos said, not looking at all sorry about it.

"Kaos... you can't just use your powers like that, dude," Kire joined in.

"Even I think that's pretty messed up," Amberly agreed.

"We look out for each other, don't we?" Kaos asked coolly.

"Each other? So you got the money for Trace?" Rose asked.

Kaos just shrugged in reply.

"It was an emergency," he explained.

"What are you talking about? Didn't you just get a boatload of money from the fight?" Ross asked him.

"Yeah, but Rezin took it."

"You expect me to believe that? That Rezin needs money? Get real, Trace."

"He did!" Trace yelled. "He took it to screw with me. I needed that money, Rose."

"If you need money that badly, why can't you just get a job like anyone else?"

"Getting money this way is so much funner," Kaos answered for

Trace. "The fighting. The casual manipulating. It's exciting. Jobs are boring."

"Sounds like something a spoiled rich kid would say," Rose grumbled.

"What did you just call me?" Kaos snapped. He had his crown on his head even then, and with Trace having seen what he did yesterday to abuse his powers, he began wondering whether his friend was going to manipulate some girls to beat up on Rose. She was brave to mess with him with his crown being on. He couldn't manipulate *her*, but he could manipulate everyone around her.

Rose fell silent, but the scowl didn't leave her face.

"You shouldn't use your powers that way," Kire said.

"It *was* a bit reckless," Amberly joined in.

"You guys are seriously giving me this crap right now?" Kaos asked. "Well, I'm not gonna deal with it. I was helping Trace. So get over it." And with that, he stood and walked away from the table.

"I can't believe you would let him do that," Rose said to Trace.

"Was it your idea?" Amberly asked.

"No!" Trace snapped. "I had no idea he was going to do that. Not until it was already happening."

"You could have stopped him," Kire said.

"I... I couldn't. You guys wouldn't get it. And I'm not gonna sit here trying to explain myself to you. I agree with you all that it wasn't right the way we went about it. But I needed that money."

Amberly was staring after Kaos. "I have to admit, I am a bit worried about him."

"Because he's letting his power get to his head?" Kire asked.

Amberly nodded. "He's the only one who is continuously using his powers for things that aren't related to what we're supposed to be using them for. But it's easy to do because it's harder for anyone to notice that he's using them. I can't exactly go around swinging punches with my gauntlet and lifting teachers by their ankles when they annoy me."

"I use mine a little," Rose admitted. "But mainly to grow plants. I don't think I'm harming much."

"Halo still won't even talk to me after saving us yesterday," Kire said. "I guess she really meant it when she said it was gonna take her a long time to charge after that."

"Well, when she does finally talk to you again, will you try to get more out of her?" Amberly asked.

"Yeah," Trace agreed. "It's not fair that even with our gifts, we have to continuously do all the searching to get any answers."

"I'll try my best," Kire said, not sounding at all confident.

"And Trace," Amberly continued. It was strange to have her finally looking at him. But he was glad for it. "You need to talk to him." She nodded her head in the direction of where Kaos went.

"Why do I gotta talk to him?" Trace complained. "He'll probably listen to you better."

"I highly doubt that. You're his best friend."

"Trace, Kaos has always been a manipulative person," Rose added. "And now he has *real* power. If something isn't done about it, that power is going to go to his head, and he is going to take advantage. And it won't be good for anyone."

They were right. Trace didn't want Kaos to pull another stunt like he had at the corner store yesterday. But how could he convince him to not use his powers like that without making him angry?

Kaos seldom took orders from anyone.

"Besides," Rose added. "I can see it on his face. If he uses that crown too much, it will weaken him severely. And that's not going to do us any good when it comes time to use our gifts during a fight."

"You mean he'll start being like *you*?" Kire asked. "With the nose bleeds and fainting and stuff?"

"It makes sense," Amberly said. "You guys all saw him. He looked tired."

"And weaker," Trace added.

"So, you'll get him to stop then, Trace?" Rose asked.

"I…"

"You have to," Rose said.

"Fine." For them, he would try. But already, he knew this talk wasn't going to go well at all.

Economics, the last class of the day, was the only class that contained all of the quintets except for Amberly. As they sat in their desks, Trace trying, but failing miserably, to pay attention to the lecture Mrs. Wright was giving, he could feel Rose's eyes burning a hole into the back of his head. More than once, he turned around to glare at her. What did she expect him to do? Interrupt Mrs. Wright's lecture so that she could talk to Kaos *right* now? Besides, he still needed to work out what it was he was going to say to him. If only he could find a way to make Kaos think it was his own idea to stop using his powers in a bad way. If Kaos thought he came up with the idea himself, he'd be more likely to listen.

Trace also felt bad because it was thanks to Kaos that he had the medicine for his mom. Even now, he could already tell she was feeling better. The entire time he got ready for school that morning, he hadn't heard her cough once.

And if she *was* drinking, she was hiding it from him?

The phone inside of the classroom rang, and Mrs. Wright paused to go over and answer it. Glad for the interruption, the class around Trace erupted into chatter.

"What do you think?" Kaos asked Trace. "Should I manipulate her to let us all watch a movie instead of listening to her drone on?" He chuckled.

Trace let out a weak laugh, too. "Actually, Kaos, about that..."

As Kaos waited, Mrs. Wright, having not even said anything to whoever was on the phone, hung it up. When she turned back to the class, Trace caught sight of the ghostly expression on her face. No one else seemed to notice since they were all busy talking with each other.

"What?" Kaos asked when Trace didn't finish his sentence.

But still, Trace couldn't answer him. Why did Mrs. Wright have that look on her face? Who had been on the phone?

"Children, children," she said urgently. "We are going into lockdown."

This shut everyone up quickly. Fumbling with her keys, Mrs. Wright hurried over and locked the classroom door. She motioned for everybody to get up from their desks and sit along the back wall. She turned the lights off.

"What's going on?"

"Is it real or just a drill?" someone else asked.

"Stay quiet," Mrs. Wright ordered.

Kaos, Trace, Kire, and Rose all sat together. "Do you guys think this is real?" Trace asked in a whisper, hoping Mrs. Wright wouldn't shush them.

"What if it's..."

Trace knew what she was asking.

What if it was Rezin?

"If it is, then we shouldn't just be sitting here," Trace said. "We have to protect the school, right?"

"He wouldn't come here now like this, would he?" Kire asked, swallowing audibly.

"He's been unpredictable lately," Rose said.

"I just got a text update from one of the other teachers," Mrs. Wright said to everyone in a quiet voice. "There is a suspect on campus. They don't look armed, but it's an adult male. They don't know who he is, where he came from, or what he's doing here."

The gang looked at each other. "It has to be him," Kire whispered.

"Let's go fight," Trace said quickly. His sword was in Kaos's locker. And he wanted desperately to let out some of his pent-up aggression. What better way than to take it out on Rezin? And maybe this time, they could finally defeat him.

"But we don't know," Rose whispered.

Trace looked at Kaos, who had his eyes closed and was gripping his crown on his head. When his eyes snapped back open, he nodded solemnly. "It's him."

"Mrs. Wright isn't going to let us just leave," Rose complained.

"Um, *hello*?" Kaos said to her, pointing at his head. He got to his feet.

"Kaos, you need to sit down," Mrs. Wright said.

"Kire, Trace, Rose, and I need to leave," Kaos said to her in a clear voice.

"Fine. Go if you must."

The other kids murmured in shock. And Trace didn't blame them. Teachers were not supposed to let students leave the class-room during a lockdown.

Trace walked out into the hall—the door was only locked on the outside—and the others had no choice but to follow, leaving their classmates stunned and confused.

"I need to get my sword out of your locker," Trace said to Kaos, all of them walking quickly through the hall.

"I was thinking," Rose said, trailing behind. "Rezin's p attacks are frequent and chaotic. Do you think… maybe he is worried we figured out the other way to stop Yash from coming here? Or maybe… maybe he was ordered to kill us before Yash arrives, and so Rezin is growing desperate because there's not much time left?"

"But we haven't figured out anything yet," Kaos said. They arrived at his locker. "Trace, go ahead. I need to concentrate." He turned away from the group and put his hands on his crown again. He was probably trying to locate where Rezin was.

Knowing his locker combo, Trace entered it and snapped the door open. He drew his sword out quickly but froze immediately afterward.

"Trace?" Kire asked. "Do you have it?"

Trace didn't answer. Panic had washed over him.

"Trace?" Rose joined in.

Slowly, Trace turned around to them. "Amberly's gauntlet isn't in here."

Just then, to their left, where the double doors to the cafeteria were, there was a loud banging noise, followed by a scream. It was one Trace knew well. It was one that made even Kaos stop what he was doing to snap his head in the direction of it. Then, at the same time, they both yelled out, "Amberly!"

The teens took off running toward the cafeteria. Thankfully, the doors weren't locked when they all burst through them. Inside, Amberly was slowly picking herself up from the ground several feet away from where a tall, average-looking man Trace had never seen before, wearing sunglasses, stood on top of a lunch table, cackling.

"Halo, you gotta wake up now," Kire said to his book, which he had pulled out of his backpack before they all left the classroom. "You've got to be ready to save us."

"Amberly," Trace called when he saw the pained expression on her face. Rezin had hurt her. He moved to go help her up and make sure she was okay, but before he could get anywhere, a chair flew into his abdomen, knocking him back.

"I've been waiting for you all," Rezin said, laughing.

Trace had no idea who his disguise was. He could be anyone. Some random stranger from the streets.

Kaos ran to help Amberly out instead. "Are you crazy?" he asked her.

She ignored Kaos, picked the chair up with her powers, and threw it back in Rezin's direction. Around them, Trace saw the cafeteria was a wreck. Tables were knocked over and broken. Trash cans lay on their sides, discarded food pouring out. Some of the windows were shattered. It was as if Rezin had gone on a rampage, destroying the room just for the fun of it.

"The police are going to be here any minute," Kire yelled to Rezin. "Do you really think this is such a good idea?"

Rezin didn't answer. Instead, he threw a glowing blue ball of electricity at Kaos, and Trace barely dodged it in time with the flat side of his sword's blade before it could smack into his friend. His sword shook with the electric energy shooting through it, the fire on it weakening briefly. Then, yelling out, he charged at Rezin. He jumped up onto the table, slashing his sword wildly through the air. "Come on, fight me!"

Rezin floated into the air. "You're no match for me. None of you are."

Trace hardly listened. All he could think about was how Rezin had hurt Amberly, and he needed to pay. He continued slashing his sword into the air, trying to reach Rezin floating above him. And then he swung his sword in just the way that made a small ball of fire shoot out of it at him. It hit Rezin, and he dropped to the ground, but in seconds, he disappeared entirely. Trace didn't even know if the fireball had hurt him. If it had done any damage at all to him.

Suddenly, Rose cried out. Even though Rezin was nowhere to be found, Rose was lifted into the air.

"What's happening to me?!" Kire yelled. Trace looked over at him, and Kire appeared to be running, but he was held in place, as if on an invisible treadmill. It had to be Rezin's doing,

Yelling out in anger, Amberly started lifting chair after chair and throwing it around the room with her kinetic abilities, as if she were trying to hit Rezin but with no idea where he was since he had turned invisible.

Trace tried to make it over to Rose, but Rezin threw her into one of the unshattered windows, using so much force that her body broke through it, and she fell to the ground outside.

"Rose!" Kire yelled. None of them could see her now.

"To the left, Amberly!" Kaos called as Amberly kept throwing chairs with her gauntlet. Kaos was using his crown to figure out Rezin's location.

Amberly hurled a chair in that direction, her chest heaving rapidly with her exertion.

"Show yourself!" Trace yelled. He ran in the direction Kaos was calling out, slicing his sword repeatedly, hoping to make contact with Rezin.

The sound of police sirens rang through the air, and when Trace looked out the broken window, he saw multiple cop cars arriving at the school.

There was a loud bang. Trace snapped his head and saw Rezin in full figure again, crashing into one of the lunch tables. Trace ran in his direction, yelling, furious, ready to kill him, but then he stopped short.

On top of the table, the sunglasses had fallen from Rezin's eyes. And they weren't balls of fire. They were regular, dark brown eyes.

And the body before him was groaning in pain as it slowly sat up, holding its head. "W-what happened?" he uttered in a groggy, pained voice.

"No way," Trace breathed.

He had been about to stop that guy. To slice him into pieces with his sword. But the person before him was no longer Rezin. At the arrival of the police, Rezin had fled, but he left behind the body he had been possessing, leaving *him* to take the fall.

IT WAS the dead of night. Trace, Amberly, Kire, and Kaos all stood huddled together outside of the hospital, calling up to Rose.

When Rose had been flung out the window by Rezin at school, she suffered injuries. Broken bones and cuts that needed stitches. It had been so bad that she was rushed to the hospital before anyone could do anything about it. Trace and Amberly had managed to hide their magical gifts before the police arrived on the scene, and it had been scary at first when the officers detained them, but they were let go once the officers had asked all of their questions and understood that they weren't the causes of the lockdown—they were only trying to help.

But, like the rest of the quintets, Rose had healing powers. All of her injuries would be gone soon, and once her bandages were pulled back and inspected by the medical professionals, she would be found out. They would *all* be found out.

So they were there to break her out.

"You can do it, Rose!" Kire called out. Rose had slid the window of her hospital room open and was looking down at them nervously. "You're sure no cameras can see?" she asked.

"Yes," Amberly growled. "Hurry up before a nurse comes into your room!"

Still looking afraid, Rose used her abilities to manipulate the tree they were all standing under. One of its branches extended up to her window and created a large arm thick enough for her to climb onto and saddle like a horse.

The rest of the gang had had quite a night already, first with breaking into the school to destroy the camera footage from their battle with Rezin in the cafeteria and to collect their gifts. They had no idea where Rezin was now, nor did they have any idea how to finally defeat him, but because of him, some poor innocent man whose body he had possessed was sitting in jail. Like the guy in the corner store, whom Kaos had manipulated, this one was claiming he had no idea what happened or why he had been in their school.

Slowly, Rose lowered herself to the branch from her window and touched down on the ground. Immediately, Kire hugged her. "Are you all right?" he asked as the tree shrunk back to its normal size.

"I'm fine," she said. But she had not looked fine when they loaded her up into that ambulance. Trace wouldn't soon forget the sight of it. Rose's body bent in an unnatural angle. Unconscious. Bleeding heavily. Literal *glass* sticking out of different parts of her body.

He shuddered.

"What am I going to do when they find out that I ran off?" Rose asked.

"Just tell them that hospitals make you uncomfortable and you didn't want to be there anymore," Amberly suggested. "Then, when they try to look at you again, just don't consent to it."

She nodded but still looked worried.

"Let's get out of here," Trace urged. Rose was still weak, her wounds not fully healed, her bones still on the mend, so he and Kire put their arms around her and helped her walk. When they reached Kire's house, Kire snuck her inside of it and wished them all goodnight. Amberly stood outside, her arms crossed as she glared up at the house.

"Are you okay?" Trace asked, knowing she didn't like being there because this was the home her father never let her be a part of.

"Don't do that, Trace," she said, shaking her head.

"Do what?"

"It's not your job to worry about me anymore."

Amberly hadn't been in the classroom when the lockdown was first called. Her last class of the day was Yearbook, and she had been walking around campus snapping photos. She had received a text from one of her classmates about the lockdown being in effect, and Amberly claimed she just had this *awful* feeling she knew it was Rezin, so she went to Kaos's locker, got her gauntlet out and hunted Rezin down. She had only arrived inside the cafeteria a few minutes before the others.

Her words stung Trace. He wanted to tell her, right then and there, that he *wanted* it to be his job to worry about her. Nothing would stop him from worrying about her for the rest of his life, even if they weren't together.

"Amberly," Kaos said before Trace could get any words out. "Let me walk you home. I know your house is in the opposite direction, but I don't want you out here alone."

"What about Trace?" Amberly asked.

Kaos looked at him. "You're good on your own, right?"

Trace cleared his throat and wiped the disappointment from his face. "Oh, yeah. I'll see you guys later."

He tried to give Amberly one last look to show he didn't want her to go. But it didn't matter.

Because she turned around and started walking away with Kaos anyway.

Chaotic. That was the perfect way to describe the next day to Trace. Everything felt so out of control with Rezin acting so out of character, attacking them at every chance he got. Not caring about the destruction he left in his wake. Making innocent people act as the culprits, wiping their memory and leaving them with no way to explain how they didn't do it afterward.

And there was nothing any of the quintets could do about it, either. They knew that the person's body that Rezin took over was innocent. But they couldn't explain any of that without exposing such a huge secret—more than likely getting called 'crazy' over it and locked away in a loony bin somewhere.

When Trace and the others arrived at school the next day, they banded together before entering. There were news vans everywhere. People were smiling and waving at them. Some were taking pictures. Trace's mom already informed him as he was getting ready earlier that their rescue was all over the news. Everyone thought them heroes. And it made Trace feel crappy. Because what they *didn't* know was that they were the reason their school was intruded upon in the first place. They were the reason why their lunchroom lay in practically ruins.

"This is insane," Rose said as all five quintets stepped inside the school together. Trace was used to being stared at because of his popularity and his menacing traits, and more recently because of his newfound solohood. But this was a whole new level. He felt *literally* famous.

"I bet this is overwhelming for you, huh, Rose?" Amberly asked with almost a sneer. As they all walked through the halls, she kept her head held high while Rose had bright red cheeks and kept looking at her feet.

"How could it not be?" Kire said in her defense.

"I'm used to it," Amberly replied. She smiled at some classmates and flipped some hair over her shoulder. "They love us. We're heroes."

Trace almost wanted to argue with her about how it didn't feel like it. But for once, he thought before he spoke. And he knew arguing with her would not be the way to win her back.

Kaos seemed to be loving it, too. It felt similar to being back in the Albus realm when the villagers cheered them on. Trace felt he would have also loved the attention—in the past. But it all felt so wrong now. So misplaced. He felt guilty. Who knew how much it was going to cost to make the repairs to the cafeteria?

Why am I even thinking about that? he asked himself. *Why do I even care?*

It continued on that way up into first period. And then, to Trace's horror and dread, his teacher, Mrs. Goody, announced that class was going to end early because there was going to be an assembly held in the gym that would last through the first part of their next class, too. When she called on Amberly, whose hand immediately shot up in the air after the announcement, Amberly asked, "What is the assembly for?"

Trace already had a feeling he knew what.

She smiled wide at them. "Why, it's for you and your friends, of course! The mayor is coming. It's a pretty big deal. A very scary thing happened in our school yesterday. And who knows what would've happened without you five?"

I know what would've happened, Trace thought. *The school would have been fine without us. It only got wrecked because of us.*

They were excused to the assembly. And since he shared his first period with everyone out of the quintets except for Rose, he walked with the other three, trying to keep his head down and blend in. But when he entered the gym, he saw that not only was it full of all of their classmates, but there were a lot of adults in attendance as well. Not just the teachers and faculty. But parents.

Their parents.

And as shocked as Trace was to see it, even his mother was here. She waved at him, looking weak and tired but still vibrant and excited.

"Oh God," Kire groaned. "My *parent* is here."

"Mine too," Trace said as they all went to take their seats. Somehow, in the throng of students, Rose found them as well.

"Oh, our father is here?" Amberly asked. "Fantastic."

Trace could sense the heavy sarcasm rolling off her.

When everyone was seated and the assembly began, it started off with the principal, Mr. Schaeffer, giving some boring speech as a bit of an introduction to who everyone was *really* most excited to hear from. The mayor of Montgomery.

The room broke into applause as the mayor took the floor, looking cartoonish in his white suit, matching hat, and dirty blonde handlebar mustache. He was short and stout and had deeply tanned skin, the white suit only making it look tanner. When he spoke, his voice was oddly high. It didn't match his look.

"First, I would just like to say to all of the students and their families that I am deeply sorry for the attack on our school that occurred yesterday," the mayor said. He spoke in a grave voice, but it was hard to take seriously with its pitch. "We should have stopped it before it even began. And we will be strengthening security immediately to ensure that something like this never happens again."

A lot of the crowd broke into curious chatter, a lot of them asking questions.

The mayor used his hands to motion for everyone to lower their voices. "I'm sure you'll have a lot of questions," he said. "I still do, as well. I am working closely with the police to figure out how this happened and what the intention of the intruder was when he happened upon our beautiful campus. You will all be updated as I am. We will get to the bottom of this, I assure you. But the purpose of this assembly today, which Mr. Schaeffer was so kind to put on on such short notice, isn't to talk about what happened yesterday. It's to honor the five students who braved the madness and stopped the attacker before things got too out of hand. Kire Hunter, Trace Henderson, Kaos Miles, Amberly McHenry, and Charlie Rose, why don't you go ahead and stand up for us?"

As much as Trace didn't want to, he followed his friends and got to his feet with them. And the entire room burst into loud applause and cheers. Trace smiled sheepishly, catching the look on his mom's face again in the crowd. She seemed so proud. So excited. Trace wondered whether or not she was sober.

After the applause settled, the mayor went on to discuss safety and to give everyone a lecture about stranger danger. Some half hour later, the students were released to go to second period.

However, the quintets had to stay behind to shake the mayor's and the principal's hands, as well as speak to their parents.

"I'm so proud of you, honey," Trace's mom said, giving him a giant hug after he shook the principal's hand. Off to the side, he could see the other quintets talking to their parents. Amberly continually side-eyed her father as she chatted with her aunt Lydia. Her father, Kire's father, Gerald Hunter, looked like he would rather be anywhere else. The scowl on his face looked permanent. He avoided eye contact with everyone. Continuously, he glanced down at his watch.

"Kids, parents, if you could all gather," Principal Schaeffer said as the mayor waved goodbye.

The quintets gathered around, their parents standing behind them.

"I just have to say, while it was very brave, what you all did, sneaking out of your classes during a lockdown, is against school rules," Mr. Schaeffer said. "You put yourself in *real* danger. If anything had happened to you kids, it would have fallen on *me*. Do you understand?"

"*I* didn't sneak out of class," Amberly said. "I was already in the hallway when that guy got here."

He looked at her briefly and then narrowed his eyes. "Still," he said, "you took a great risk. And I don't want the rest of the students to think you're setting an example. I don't want any of them to think it's okay to leave class during a lockdown like that if it happens again. God forbid, of course."

"I don't think they need to be lectured," Amberly's aunt, Lydia, spoke up. "They were heroes. Yes, it was dangerous and rather stupid, if you want my honest opinion, for them to go at him themselves, but in the end, they did put a stop to that psycho."

The other parents murmured their agreement. Even Gerald Hunter.

Principles Shaeffer must have felt overruled by all of them, for he crossed his arms and let out a sigh. "Very well. I just thought I would be the one to remind you that being a hero is not more important than being safe."

"The way I see it, Mr. Schaeffer," Trace said, surprising himself for speaking out. "If everyone was worried about only protecting themselves, then who would have saved us?"

19

When Trace stepped outside that Saturday, he found clear skies. No smoke in the atmosphere. No ash falling into his hair.

The fire in The White Forest had finally been extinguished.

At this news, he awoke to text in the quintet group chat, where they all decided they should go back to the Albus realm and continue cleaning up the mess that they had made. And according to Kire, who was informed by Halo, Albus's funeral was going to be held today in the magical realm.

The gang was still getting a lot of attention from the media for their heroic saving of their high school. It was hard to sneak away from their families and houses and meet up with each other at the edge of the woods. They were worried about being followed. About being caught with their gifts. What would the media think of Trace's sword and Amberly's strange gauntlet? They looked a bit ridiculous, like they were about to go play make-believe with each other with some theater props from backstage at their auditorium at school.

It was still somewhat early in the day, and a lot of the teens were just waking up, so they didn't have a lot to discuss as they trekked through the burnt-up, charred remnants of the forest. Several times, as they made their way to the cave, there would be nothing but the burnt, dead graveyard of tree trunks to one side of them and a perfect, lush green forest, looking as if nothing ever happened, to the other side of them. The entire forest hadn't been burned down, and Trace was incredibly grateful. Even more so that Rose had her gift and could spring up new plants here and there as they walked along. She didn't overdo it, though, because she knew she needed to preserve her energy for cleaning up the Albus realm.

Once the gang arrived back in the Albus realm, it was another clear, beautiful, sunny day, much like it had been back in their world. For the first time, both worlds having blue skies gave Trace a strange feeling of hope. That, and whenever Amberly found herself walking beside Trace accidentally, she didn't recoil and scurry away to go stand beside Kaos instead.

They used their magical stone to teleport to the next town because they still had some time before the funeral started. Trace fully expected that they would have to re-explain themselves to all of the villagers about why they were there, why they were dressed so strangely, who they were, and what they wanted. But, it appeared that as time passed, the word had spread like wildfire through all of the villages and hamlets, and everybody knew who they were and knew to expect them.

They were greeted with smiles, applause, and handshakes. Lots of men and women were eager to get to work with them, and tons of little kids were excited to see their magical abilities first-hand.

Trace enjoyed himself thoroughly. He met a little boy who couldn't be older than eight, who was fascinated with his sword. Trace loved showing him all the things he could do with it, and the little boy thought it was the coolest thing in the world when the fire snaked around Trace's arm but didn't affect him.

It seemed every time Trace came back to the Albus realm, he remembered how much he loved it and how much he dreaded going back to Earth. He liked being here, where he had a purpose and where he could put himself to work.

It was almost easy to forget he was heartbroken about Amberly and stressed about his sick, alcoholic mother.

Albus's funeral was to be held in the forest near where his house was, so when the time came, the group teleported to the great treehouse. There, they saw no one was home, but there were signs pointing in the direction they needed to go to get to the funeral. And when they all arrived at a clearing among all of the thick trees, they were amazed at how many people had shown up to say goodbye to Albus. There were all sorts of beings, magical and not, wearing all sorts of different garbs and styled outfits, all clashing together in a delightful and colorful way. There were no chairs; everyone stood before Albus's wooden casket, with a gap down the middle of the crowd creating an aisle. Everyone looked pleased to see the quintets there. Gertrude and the other Albus were standing at the front by the casket, and Gertrude smiled warmly at them though her eyes were bloodshot. Albus gave a low head nod. The casket was closed. They would not be seeing Albus's body, and Trace was relieved.

The service started, and as they all stood among the crowd, Trace found himself next to Amberly once more. He thought about her mother and how Amberly had just been to a funeral for her not long ago.

"Are you doing okay?" he asked in a quiet voice so that he wouldn't interrupt the service.

Amberly looked at him as if she were unsure whether or not he was talking to her. When she seemed to realize that he was, she bit her bottom lip. "I guess," she said. "I don't know."

"It's okay if you're not," he told her. "Is it bringing up memories of your mom?"

"That, and… It's just sad in general. I mean, all of these people are pleased to see us, but we're the reason Albus is dead. Just like at school. With Rezin."

"Wait, *you* felt weird about being congratulated at school, too?" Trace had thought he was the only one.

She shrugged. "Not that I was going to admit it... until now, I guess." She chuckled a bit. But then, the strangest thing happened, and her shoulders crumpled. And Amberly began to cry.

Trace wanted to comfort her. He wanted to make her feel better. He even lifted up his arm to put it around her, but he hadn't been quick enough. On the other side of her, Kaos quickly enveloped her in a hug. She buried her head in his shoulder and cried as the service continued.

It nearly broke Trace's heart all over again to see it. *He* should be hugging Amberly. Not Kaos.

He cleared his throat and faced forward, pretending neither of them were beside him at all.

The service was sad, but it was also nice, in Trace's opinion. He got to learn a lot about Albus and the type of man that he was. A lot of people spoke, sharing sweet stories and memories of him. Apparently, Albus was quite the comedian. He made a lot of dark times a little bit brighter for many people.

When the service was over, and the casket was lowered into the ground and covered with dirt by a group of other Albuses, all looking shockingly alike, the crowd broke apart into little groups, talking with one another. A lot of them were curious to meet The Unlikely Defenders, and it kept Trace plenty occupied for quite some time as he shook hands and learned many names he would surely forget in an instant.

When he turned away from a short, frumpy little woman named Zaravina, he bumped into someone. "Oh, sor—"

It was Amberly. They had bumped into each other at the same time, both turning away from someone else.

They laughed awkwardly. But Trace was glad to see she was no longer crying.

"Um," Amberly said, grabbing her elbow with the opposite hand, "do you think we should try to talk to Albus and Gertrude again? See if they can tell us anything else about what Albus left for us?"

"It could be worth a try," Trace said. "I actually wanted to see if they would let us search their house. If maybe whatever Albus left for us is somewhere in there."

"That's a good idea, Trace."

For a moment, they were both silent, just staring at each other.

Then Amberly started turning away.

But Trace wasn't done. There was something else he needed to say. Gently, he took her hand and turned her back around. She didn't recoil. She didn't snatch it away. She just looked confused. Curious.

"Just really quick," Trace said, feeling flustered and a bit nervous. "I just wanted to know something."

"What is it?"

"I want to know if you've realized that your life is important yet."

I... Oh." Amberly was apparently at a loss for words.

"It does matter, Amberly. I'm sorry I didn't show it more, but your life might be one of the only ones that truly matters to me."

Trace didn't want her to feel like she had to say anything back to that. So he gave her a weak smile and then led the way to the rest of the quintets.

Together, he and Amberly told them their plan, and then they all stood to the side and waited for Gertrude to finish talking to others. She noticed them waiting and excused herself to greet them.

"I know it means the world to Albus that you came," she said to them. She was wearing a purple gown so dark it was nearly black, and she wore a unique purple silk hat with black netting covering half of her face. When she spoke, her voice was somber.

"We wouldn't have missed it for the world," Trace said, hanging his head a bit. "It was a nice service."

"It was. Um... so... Gertrude," Amberly said awkwardly, "we

were wondering if it would be possible to maybe search your tree-house for that item Albus left behind for us?"

The other Albus, the one that had been comforting Gertrude, who was great friends with *their* Albus, arrived in their little circle. Gertrude gently placed a hand on his shoulder. "Do you think what Albus left them could possibly be inside my very treehouse?" she asked him.

Albus clasped his hands together in front of himself. "I suppose that could be possible."

Gertrude nodded at them. "Then, by all means, help yourself. I have nothing to hide. And I'll admit, I haven't gone through Albus's things yet. It's much too soon for me. Too hard. If you find what it is you believe you need, take it."

Thanking her, the quintets went into the treehouse and began their search.

"I can't believe how incredible this place is," Rose said. "When I have my own house someday, I want it to look just like this."

"People would think you are crazy," Amberly told her. "There is probably not a single house in the world that looks like this one. It wouldn't fit in. Especially if you stayed in Montgomery."

"I have no desire to stay there," she said.

"You don't?" Kire asked, overhearing them as he searched in the kitchen. Trace was checking the closet under the stairs. So far, all he could find was a bunch of old books and boxes that looked to be full of random assortments of things. Nothing looked like it would be of any significance to them.

"No way," Rose said to Kire. "There's too much of the world to see."

"Huh."

"What?" she asked him.

"I guess I just never even thought about where I wanted to go in the future."

"I think it would be cool to stay here," Trace said. He liked it in the Albus realm.

"But you wouldn't really," Amberly chimed in.

"I wouldn't?"

"You—you couldn't," she said, stopping in her search through the cupboards in the kitchen next to her half brother. " Trace, this isn't your world. You don't... You don't belong here."

She seemed completely appalled that Trace would even have the thought.

"I know that," he said. "I'm just saying—it would be cool."

She pursed her lips and continued searching.

An hour later, the teens felt they hadn't found anything inside the beautiful treehouse. It had been searched from top to bottom. Feeling discouraged, Trace joined the others in gathering in the foyer. Through the opened front door, Trace watched Gertrude and Albus saying goodbye to the remaining guests outside the gate of the front yard.

What other places can we search?

"I just don't know where it would be," Kire said, pulling his hair, apparently having the same thought as Trace.

"Or what it would even *be* that we need to search *for*," Rose added. "What if we did find it here, but we just didn't know it was what we needed? It's all so confusing."

"Let's just go," Kaos said. He had been oddly silent most of the time they searched.

"Are you okay?" Amberly asked him.

He nodded but didn't speak. He just started walking outside. So, since he was supposedly their leader, the others followed him.

"Any luck?" Gertrude asked when they approached her and Albus at the gate.

"Unfortunately not," Kaos said, standing tall in front of them. "But we won't stop searching. We will find it... eventually." He sounded confident, but Trace wondered if he actually felt it.

"What if we don't?" Rose asked behind him. She was at least being honest. She felt hopeless. Trace sort of did, too. They didn't even know what they were looking for, so how were they supposed to find it?

"You shouldn't lose hope," Albus told them. "If I knew Albus as well as I think I did, then I would be able to tell you that it is there somewhere, just waiting for you to find it. And maybe... just maybe, Albus put it somewhere that he knew you would be able to retrieve it when the time was right. When you need the object to the most."

The gang all looked at each other. Then Trace squinted and turned his head back to Albus. "Are you *sure* you don't know what it is? Aren't all of your minds connected? Do you maybe actually know the truth, and you just don't want to tell us?"

Albus smiled at him. It was a strained, strange smile. "I am sorry, Trace. If only it were that easy."

Yeah, Trace thought, side-glancing at Amberly, who he caught staring at him before she quickly looked away. *If only*.

The next day, after a quiet morning at his home, Trace answered a call from Kaos, who told him to meet him at Stoneridge Park, a park that was within walking distance, falling right in the middle between Trace's house and Kaos's.

Trace, bikeless still because his was at Kaos's house, walked to the park, taking his time with the stroll because of the beautiful weather. It was as if a huge weight had been lifted off his shoulders now that the fire was put out in The White Forest. He felt terrible for starting it, and knowing that a lot of the forest was destroyed still made his heart ache, but he was also glad that Rose had her ability. He would have to talk to her and ask her about continuing the reforestation in her spare time if she could.

Kaos was already at the park when Trace arrived. He practically jumped off the bench he was sitting on when he saw Trace, a huge grin on his face. The crown was on his head. Trace, not worried about getting in trouble for carrying it around here, wore his sword in its scabbard on his hip. They didn't have school today, and Trace felt better and more protected against Rezin when he kept it on himself. If only he could get away with wearing the sword around school like Kaos could wear his crown.

"Hey," Trace said when they reached each other.

"I have good news," Kaos told him.

Trace was uncertain about the look on his friend's face. 'Good news' to Kaos could mean something entirely different from what it meant to Trace. They used to be more in sync. But lately, ever since they had become defenders of the earth, things had been different. Trace had been changing. Kaos was maybe changing, too, but not in a way that did anybody any good.

"What is it?" Trace asked. "Did you find what Albus left behind?"

What if he found it yesterday and didn't want to tell the others for some reason?

Kaos rolled his eyes. "Just forget about that. I'm sick of always worrying about Rezin and the other realm. Don't you ever just want life to go back to the way it was before?"

Trace thought immediately of Amberly. "Yeah." He shoved his hands in his pockets. "A lot."

"For a moment, let's pretend life *is* the way it was before." Kaos slapped a hand on his shoulder. "I've set up another fight."

"A... A fight?" Trace stepped back, Kaos's hand falling off his shoulder. "What do you mean?"

"For money! It'll be right here in the park!"

The smile on his face—it registered with Trace now what it meant. It was his sinister smile, indicating he was up to no good.

"Dude," Trace complained. "The last time we did this, the person I was fighting was Rezin. You don't think that maybe that'll just happen all over again if we have another one?"

The last thing Trace wanted to do was have another fight with some random person and risk another confrontation with Rezin, where he would have to fight against him without using any powers.

"I considered it," Kaos said. "And if some guy shows up wearing sunglasses, we will find a reason to cancel it. Simple as that. In the last fight, we didn't quite realize yet that Rezin always has the sunglasses on. Even when he is disguised as somebody else. It's his telling sign. This will be different, Trace. The kid I found goes to a different school. Sunset High. Some people messaged me on social media because they saw videos online of some of your other fights. This kid is pretty big, but I don't think he has any real skill. I think it will be an easy one."

Trace shook his head. "I don't want to do another fight, Kaos."

Kaos looked at him as if he were speaking another language. "What are you talking about?"

"You heard me," Trace said. He was trying not to get mad at his friend, but the irritation grew nonetheless. "I'm not doing it. Count me out."

"You can't just *not* do it, Trace," Kaos said. "I already set it up."

"Without talking to me about it?" Trace asked. "I'm not fighting anyone."

"Then how are you going to get the money for the medicine?" Kaos snapped, sounding angry. "Don't expect me to rob any more stores for you."

"I didn't even want to do that in the first place!"

"Oh, *please*."

Trace clenched his fists. "I didn't know what you were planning on doing that day. I didn't know *that* was how you were going to get the money. Aren't you *tired* of causing trouble? Kaos, don't you remember anything Albus had told us? I know I do—I'm not supposed to be having these random fights anymore. I'm not supposed to be a huge jerk to everyone all of the time. Albus made it pretty clear that that is how I will get stronger with my power."

Kaos rolled his eyes. "Come on. It doesn't matter who you are outside of the group. That doesn't affect anything. All that matters is that we all get along and then our gifts work together well. Beyond all of that, you can be whatever you want to be. The Trace I know didn't get to the top of the school by being the nice guy."

"I don't care about any of that anymore."

"Yes, you do." Kaos's face clouded over. It grew darker.

"You're forgetting that your crown doesn't work on me," Trace told him. "I'm not doing this fight, Kaos."

"Go ahead and back out, Trace. See what happens."

"What are you saying?"

"You're ungrateful, Trace. I've done so much for you. Without me, your mom would probably have drunk herself to death by now."

It was a painful punch to the gut. Trace was so shocked and angered by the words from his supposed best friend that he couldn't even speak. Suddenly, he wanted to fight. Just not with the person Kaos set him up to fight with.

And before he let his anger take over and became that pressurized can of air again, he turned and stormed away from him.

"I'M REALLY glad that you backed out of it," Rose told Trace after he finished filling her and Kire in on what had happened with Kaos at the park a short while ago. The three of them were sitting inside Aunt Marg's, in the room with the tables and their frilly cloths. Trace was devouring sweet treats that Aunt Margaret had brought them. Rose and Kire were slowly sipping some tea.

Trace was miserable. He felt like everything was falling apart. His relationship with Kaos. Amberly. Who was he, this person who now hung out with Kire and Rose on his weekends, having tea and cookies inside Aunt Marg's?

Who have I become?

"Me too," Kire agreed with Rose. "There are other ways you can get the money, T."

"Yeah," Trace said after finishing another cookie. "I'm going to try and find a part-time job, as lame as it sounds. I get all of my fighting done in the Albus realm. And fixing up all those hamlets, all of that manual labor, that helps me, too. I don't need to have these fights anymore. I don't..." He couldn't believe what he was about to tell them. "I don't want to be the bad guy anymore. I've gotten a taste of what it feels like to be the hero. The good one. And I like it so much more."

Rose beamed at him. "That's really great, Trace. Seriously."

"Yeah, if only Kaos felt the same way!" Trace said, sulking.

"We need to find a way to get him to come around," Kire said. He looked away from the two of them, seemingly deep in thought. "There has to be some way that we can convince him that being a good person is better than seeking control over everyone and everything. There are other ways to get other people's respect, you know?"

"Kaos is just spoiled," Rose said. "I'm sorry, but I'm just saying it. Everyone already thinks it. He's been handed everything he's ever wanted in life. He has wealth. Parents who adore him. He doesn't know what it's like to have hardships. He's never had anything rough happen in his entire life. But us? Amberly? We've all gone through horrible things. And it's made us better people for it. As much as I don't like to admit it about Amberly. Obviously, it's terrible that her mother died, but her death *did* make her seem to realize that her priorities were out of whack."

"Can we not... bring Amberly into this?" Trace asked. His stomach rolled, and suddenly, just at the mention of her, the cookies in front of him stopped sounding good, and his hand paused right above the plate as he had been about to reach for another before Rose started babbling about his ex. He retracted his hand, no longer wanting any.

"Amberly?" Rose asked Trace. Then she shrugged. "I thought everything was okay with you two. You seemed to be pretty civil yesterday."

"Civil." Trace didn't want to be civil with Amberly. They were like a divorced couple forced to get along because of the kids they shared. Only, in this instance, the kid they shared was the gift they each possessed that brought them all together, their responsibility of being The Unlikely Defenders.

"What?" Rose asked, noticing the flat way Trace repeated her.

"Dude, just talk to her," Kire chimed in, giving Trace an encouraging nod.

How is it that I told them I don't want to talk about her, and continuing to talk about her is exactly what they're doing? Trace thought to himself.

"I have talked to her," Trace said defensively.

"Wait a second," Rose said to him. She set her teacup down on its plate rather noisily. "Are you trying to get back together with her?" Her brows furrowed deeply.

"I think they should get back together," Kire said. "Trace is clearly miserable without her."

Rose scoffed at him. "Are you *serious*?"

"What?" Trace and Kire asked her together.

"Trace," Rose snapped, eyeing him scornfully. "You are much better off without her. *Much* better off. You two were horrible for each other. You brought out the worst in each other. You guys fed off each other's toxicity."

"No way," Kire argued. "If anything, Trace kept Amberly grounded. Now she's this wild, loose animal."

"I want her back," Trace told Rose. "I... I shouldn't have broken up with her. I should have fixed things instead."

It was the first time he had said it out loud to anyone.

"Just—don't say anything to her," he demanded, his tone sharp.

"But, Trace," Rose started, "you've been doing so well."

"No, I haven't," Trace argued. "Maybe it seemed like it to you, Rose, but I haven't been doing well."

"Yeah, and Rose, with the two of them broken up, it makes it difficult for our gifts to work well together," Kire pointed out. He looked back at Trace. "You need to talk to her. Sort out your issues. Either get together again or don't, but at least find a way to become friends again. I don't really know if that's possible for you two, so you should probably just get her to take you back. I bet she would say yes."

Rose looked angered. "I can't believe you are suggesting that, Kire," she said.

Kire started to look irritated back at her. "Why not? We need our gifts to work well together. What does it matter to you if they are together or not?"

"Because they're horrible when they're together! With the two of them and Kaos... At St. Bernard High, they're pure... evil."

"You don't have to talk about me like I'm not sitting right here," Trace snapped. "Seriously, Rose. Do you really think that if I were to get back together with Amberly, we would go back to being how we were before? To treating you like dirt? To treating everyone around us like dirt? Look, I already told you, I don't wanna be the bad guy anymore. And I don't think Amberly does, either. It's Kaos. Kaos is the one you have to worry about. His crown. His gift. For the rest of us, our gifts have been making us better people. They've been improving our lives. But with Kaos... He's getting—I don't know. It's like he's getting darker or something."

Rose gnawed on her bottom lip, her eyes downcast. Kire nodded along with Trace, seeming to be in complete agreement.

Trace stood from the table and grabbed one last cookie for the road. "Look, I am dealing with too much already to keep sitting here and listening to you argue about whether or not I should be with Amberly. The fact of the matter is that we're not together right now. I want her back, but I don't know if that's going to happen. Even if I ask her, we don't know that she would accept me. I hurt her. And you know what? She hurt me, too. We both have stuff we need to figure out. So, I'm gonna go. Besides, I need to check on my mom soon."

"Is she all right?" Rose asked softly.

"She is... yeah."

Even though Trace was basically more friends with Rose and Kire these days than he was with Kaos and Amberly, he didn't feel the need to let Kire and Rose in right now about everything going on with his mom and him. He still couldn't even believe that this was how his life had changed. If someone had asked him just months ago if they ever thought he would be here right now with the two of them as friends, he would have laughed in their face.

But right now, the fact of the matter was that Rose and Kire were the only real friends Trace had.

During Trace's walk back home to his house after Aunt Marg's, his hands shoved into his pockets and his eyes down at the sidewalk, he thought about how much his life had changed recently. He thought about his animosity toward Kaos. His sadness over his breakup with Amberly. How he had grown closer with not only Kire Hunter but the weird, plant-loving chick, Charlie Rose, as well. And in all truth, Trace missed his old life. He missed his best friends and the good times they used to have together. He, Amberly, and Kaos all got along so well at one point. Even when they weren't at school. Even when they weren't trying to impress everyone and make them respect them. When it was just the three of them, at one of their houses—usually Kaos's since it was the biggest—they had fun together. They laughed. They joked around. They understood each other. They all wanted the same things. And that's what made them such a good fit.

What did Amberly want now? Had that changed like Trace sensed it had? He had been watching Amberly's behavior at school, how she had become a bit more reserved and closed off, how she seemed to stop caring as much about what she looked like in front of everyone, how she was no longer sassy and rebellious and smiling her wicked—but beautiful—smile whenever she thought up a devious plan. Was that just a temporary change while she was mourning the loss of her mother? Would the old Amberly come back? Or had everything she had gone through made the change more permanent? Maybe what Amberly and Trace both wanted had changed, but maybe it was still the same thing. Maybe they still had that in common.

Trace paused outside of the old movie theater that was still running in their small town. The only reason it was still open was more for nostalgia factors than because it was everyone's preferred place to see movies. All of the new theaters these days had those reclining seats and massive screens, and spots could be reserved ahead of time. This theater was truly old-fashioned, with folding seats squished together where you had to share an armrest with the person beside you, old projectors, and dirty screens. But the popcorn was delicious. The small theaters inside were cozy. The place showed a lot of old movies, and Trace and Amberly had gone to see a few of them together back when they were a couple.

There was a HELP WANTED sign on the window of the ticket booth.

Well... I do need a job... Trace thought, staring at the poster intensely. As much as he hated the idea of his classmates seeing him working at a place like this, he went inside the theater and spoke to the hiring manager. Really, he had just gone in to fill out an application. What he *hadn't* expected was to be hired on the spot by the old man. He had hardly even asked Trace that many questions. It seemed to Trace that he was just desperate enough for any sort that he didn't care who came in asking for the position.

So, when Trace left to resume his walk back home, he was now a part-time Montgomery Theater employee.

Why are you smiling? he thought to himself as he walked with a little more pep in his step. *You're going to hate it. Sweeping popcorn. Getting told what to do by an old, senile man.*

But he was proud of himself. He was going to make money to

afford his mom's medication. And maybe, even, he could start saving up money for himself. He didn't know what he would save up for, but he always wanted to have savings of his own. He was so used to everything he made going to help his mother.

Finally, when he arrived home, he unlocked his front door and still had that ridiculous smile on his face as he entered. His eyes went to the sofa as he closed the front door behind him, and to his surprise, his mother wasn't lounging around on it like she usually was.

"Mom?" he asked. There came no response, but in the kitchen, he heard laughter. It was his mom's laugh. But there was someone else laughing, too.

Kaos.

Trace entered the kitchen, confused as to why Kaos was at his house hanging out with his mom. If Kaos needed something, why didn't he just text Trace?

"Hi, honey!" Vivian called, sitting across from Kaos at the kitchen table. Kaos's back was to Trace. Apparently, he and Trace's mom were having a *grand* time together. Vivian's eyes were bright, shining with laughter. She had always liked Kaos. It made Trace wonder if she still would if she knew the things Kaos pressured Trace into doing.

Trace was very confused. Why was Kaos there? They were in a fight. Trace didn't want to talk to him. And he didn't think Kaos would want to talk to him, either.

"What are you guys doing?" Trace asked the pair.

"What have you got in your hand there?" Vivian asked him, ignoring his question. Trace was holding the paperwork that he needed to fill out for his new job. But he didn't want to talk about that now, *especially* in front of Kaos. He wished he could hide the fact that he got a job from him forever. He knew Kaos would judge him for it. Make fun of him. Look down on him. *Working* for money was beneath him. But why would he ever need to work when his parents gave him anything he wanted?

"Nothing," he said to his mother.

"Vivian and I were just catching up," Kaos told Trace, his back still to him.

"Why?" Trace snapped.

"Honey, what's wrong?" Vivian asked, looking surprised by Trace's abrasive behavior.

"Kaos," Trace snapped, addressing his best friend and ignoring his mother. What was Kaos trying to pull? What if he came here to dispose of his mother's medication and make it so Trace was desperate enough to get the money to replace it that he agreed to the fight after all? "What are you doing here? What do you want?"

Kaos chuckled and slowly turned around in his seat.

Stones filled in Trace's stomach, and he felt like it was going to fall right out of his butt. Not only was Kaos wearing different clothes than he had been earlier, not only was the crown missing from the top of his head, but there were sunglasses over his eyes.

It's his telling sign.

"Can't a guy come and say hi to his best friend's mom?" Kaos asked Trace. But Trace knew it wasn't Kaos in front of him. It was Rezin speaking.

"Get out," Trace commanded.

"Trace," Vivian said, her voice chastising. "What's gotten into you?"

"Get out!" Trace shouted at Rezin. Who had been in his house. Alone with his mom. Why hadn't Trace gotten home sooner? What if he had gotten home any *later*? What would Rezin have done to his mom? What was he going to do right *now*? Was he going to attack? Were Trace and his mother both in danger?

Rezin, disguised as Kaos, slowly got to his feet. "It's all right, Ms. Henderson," Kaos said, his gaze fixed on Trace. Or at least that's what it seemed like—Trace couldn't be too certain with the sunglasses and all. "Trace and I are just having... A bit of a spat."

"You don't have to go," Vivian said to him, frowning. "Whatever is going on between you two, why don't you just talk it out?"

"Not gonna happen," Trace said. "In fact, if he doesn't leave right now, things might get violent." He was tempted to get his Pentfire and fight him anyway, right here and now, one on one. He needed to protect his mother. He shouldn't have ever let her out of his sight.

"Absolutely not," Vivian said. "There will be no such thing happening under my roof."

"I'm going," Rezin replied. "Don't worry, there's no need to fight, Trace."

Trace didn't say another word. And he didn't take his eyes off Rezin the entire walk from the kitchen to the front door.

"Well, it was lovely to see you," Vivian called, waving goodbye to him.

"I really enjoyed the talking, just the two of us, one on one, Ms. Henderson," Rezin replied. "Perhaps we will do it again sometime."

Vivian giggled. She was usually charmed by Kaos. But how could she not tell right now how *unlike* Kaos his impersonator was being?

"Bye, *Kaos*," Trace glowered. He opened the front door.

"You enjoy the rest of your night, Trace," Rezin said to him as he stepped out onto the porch. "Sweet dreams."

Sweet dreams? Trace thought. It was still broad daylight out.

Trace decided not to respond. He followed Rezin out onto the porch and kept his eyes trained on him until he was far from their property and out of his sight.

When he went back inside the house, he locked the door. Then he went around to make sure all the windows were locked as well.

"What's going on?" Vivian asked, drinking something clear out of a glass as she hovered in the arch between the kitchen and living area, watching him.

"Nothing. Doesn't matter."

"It's just water, by the way."

Trace paused and looked at her.

She gave him a small smile. "I saw you staring. It's just water."

Trace wanted to feel happy to hear it. He wanted that sense of relief. But it didn't come. How could it? Several times, his mom had told him she was done drinking. It never lasted.

"Mom, you can't just let my friends inside the house when I'm not here," he told her.

"Even Kaos? Honey, the boy's like another son to me."

"I don't care," he snapped. "In fact, don't let *anyone* in unless I'm home. Montgomery's been a dangerous place to live lately. Just... keep the doors and windows locked and don't answer the door for anyone, got it?"

"Yes, sir," she said, giving him a fake salute. She wasn't taking him seriously.

Trace rolled his eyes.

"Now," she said, changing the subject, "do you want to tell me what that new-hire paperwork is all about?"

He softened a little, the pride swelling inside his chest again over how he landed himself a job. He filled his mom in on what happened at the theater. And she seemed even prouder of him than he did of himself as she hugged him and thanked him. Then they spent the rest of the evening together, and his mother even managed to cook a pretty decent dinner.

However, when the night whirled around, Trace was nervous. He couldn't stop thinking about what Rezin, in the disguise of Kaos, had said to him before he left earlier.

Sweet dreams.

Trace refused to lie down on his bed. Instead, he paced about his bedroom. His mom had already gone to sleep, for once not passing out on the sofa.

No way am I sleeping, he thought to himself as he paced. He was positive Rezin's words were a warning. If Trace went to sleep, he was going to do something to him and his dreams. He was sure of it.

When it felt like hours had passed, Trace checked the clock to find it had only been minutes. He was growing more and more tired. He had given up on the pacing and was sitting on the bedroom floor, his back up against the side of his bed. His eyes were drooping. He was exhausted from all of the work in the Albus realm yesterday. He and the other quintets were actually losing sleep because of how time worked between the realms. They had spent a whole day in the Albus realm with the funeral and the hamlet-repairing and searching Gertrude and Albus's house. And then, when they arrived back in the Earth realm, they still had the whole rest of the day there to get through as well. The jet lag was hitting Trace hard.

As much as he wanted to continue to try and fight it, sleep eventually overcame him.

And just like he knew it would, the nightmare came quickly.

Trace was encased in pitch-black darkness. It was all around him. In front of him. Below him. Above him. Not a thing was in sight. He couldn't see his hand in front of his face.

Feeling panic rising and his throat as a scream, he turned in a frantic half circle. Something caught his eye and made him freeze. What seemed to be an entire football field away, he could see what looked to be a movie set. Or maybe a TV sitcom set. There was nowhere else to go, so he knew he needed to walk toward it. His footsteps were slow at first. He kept his eyes trained on this strange sitcom set. It looked familiar. Was that... *his* furniture on the set?

There were people, too, he soon realized, inside of the space. Two people in what looked to be Trace's living room. He couldn't see the person on the couch because of the way it was staged; the couch faced the TV wall, the back of it to Trace, and the figure was sitting on it. But as he got closer, he recognized the familiar messy up-do. It was his mother.

The man standing before her, his hands on his hips across from the coffee table, looked angry. Trace didn't quite recognize him. But it didn't take him long to figure out it was his father. What his father would look like right now if Trace were to run into him on the street. How did Rezin know this? Had he tracked him down?

Trace walked a little quicker now. He didn't like the look on his father's face as he stared at his mother. He could hear him yelling at her. And he could make out the words when he drew nearer.

"You are a worthless drunk! Why did I ever waste my time with you!"

Trace still felt so far away. He started to run.

"Stop!" he called.

But to his mother and father, Trace was apparently invisible.

"I cannot believe you are the mother of my child!" his dad yelled. "Having Trace with you was such a mistake!"

"Shut up!" Tracy bellowed. His mother was yelling at his father, too. Then, the furniture started flying. Trace's father flipped over the coffee table. He flung books off shelves and knocked over glasses while Vivian screamed at him and begged him to stop.

Before Trace could get there, when he was only feet away from being able to intercept the horrific scene in front of him, it was as if an invisible pair of hands slammed into his chest, knocking him backward off his feet.

He landed on the ground on his back, the breath knocked out of him. He got up quickly, panting. The fighting, the throwing and screaming at each other, was still happening on the TV set. Trace tried again. He ran toward his father, wanting to jump on his back and get him as far away from his mother as possible.

Again, hands slammed into him and pushed him back.

"Stop!" Trace shouted furiously. He tried two more times. But it didn't matter how many times he ran toward that set. He couldn't protect his mother. He kept getting knocked backward.

How the heck can I get to them?! he thought angrily as he got to his feet yet again.

The Pentfire.

He looked down, and suddenly, there his sword was, safely in its scabbard. He pulled it out quickly, and the flames erupted.

Try to push this *back, Rezin.*

He shot fireball after fireball through the darkness toward the movie set, toward the spot where the hands kept slamming into him and pushing him back. Trace was certain the hands belonged to an invisible Rezin.

It didn't take long at all before one of the fire blasts seemed to slam into something solid before the flames disappeared altogether. Trace heard an angry yell that he thought came from his father, but maybe it hadn't. Maybe it had been from Rezin.

The next thing Trace knew, he was waking to hear his mother's screams coming from her bedroom.

Trace, who had slept on the ground of his bedroom, shot up to his feet, panting. Feeling like he couldn't move quick enough, he grabbed his Pentfire and ran to his mother.

Vivian was sitting upright in her bed, her tears mixing with sweat that was glistening on her face.

"What happened?" Trace yelled. "Where is he?" He fully expected Rezin to be there in the room with her. Or his father. What if Rezin had brought his father here to make that scene from the nightmare a reality?

"Trace!" his mother gasped. "I'm so sorry. I... I was having a really bad dream. I'm okay."

"So, no one's here?" Trace asked, releasing his hand from his sword handle.

"No. Of course not."

"What was your dream about?"

His mother stared at him, noticing what he was holding. "What is that?" she asked.

"Nothing."

"Is that... a *sword*?"

"I thought... I thought you were in danger."

"A sword?" she repeated, looking astonished.

"I know it's an interesting choice of defense weapon," he said, "but we needed to have something. And this was free."

It was the best he could come up with on such short notice.

His heartbeat calming down, Trace stepped deeper into his mother's bedroom.

"Mom, forget about the sword. What was your dream about?"

"It... It doesn't matter, Trace. I'm fine. It was just a dream. It must be the middle of the night. Go back to bed."

Trace stopped to consider for a moment, but he was quick to come to the realization that he needed to know. "Was it about Dad?"

They didn't talk about him. Not if either of them could help it. Sure, Vivian would yell at Trace about him being like his father whenever she was angry. But they never had real actual conversations about him. About what he had done to them. About how they were emotionally affected.

"How did you know that?" Vivian asked. Her question told Trace all he needed to know. She had had the same dream he had. Only, she had to live out Trace's abusive father yelling and throwing things around her. In the nightmare, she hadn't even noticed Trace was there, trying to save her.

"I... I had a dream about him, too," he explained. "Mom?"

"What?"

"I'm never going to let Dad hurt you again."

"Come here."

Trace approached his mother at her bed, and she wrapped her arms around him, forcing him to bend over and hug her back.

But he didn't mind it.

Trace thought a lot about his father when he went to school the next day. It had been so long since his father was a consistent part of his mind, since he was at the forefront of it. And it was Rezin's fault. Trace hated it when this happened. He hated reminders of his dad. He had done fine for seventeen years without hardly thinking about him. It didn't need to start now.

Besides, it's not like I'm ever going to see him again anyway.

He supposed the only good thing about being consumed by recalling the nightmare of last night was that it was a good distraction from the fact that Kaos was still not talking to him. And since things with Amberly were still weird, apparently, Kaos didn't have to worry about being caught in the middle of the two of them. He and Amberly avoided Trace, and Trace just stuck to hanging out with Kire and Rose, though he didn't say much to them. Or *anyone*, for that matter, even though he was still catching a lot of looks from the ladies.

It was only toward the end of the day, when the memories of the nightmare he had last night were finally starting to fade, that Trace grew more annoyed about Kaos. About their fight. Why was Kaos giving him the cold shoulder when Trace was the one who had more reason to be mad?

He glared at the back of his friend's head in his last class of the day. Kaos was wearing his crown as usual, and all of St. Bernard High's students and staff were just acceptant of it. Sometimes, Trace thought it would have been nice if Kaos could use his gift on the other quintets. Kaos would be able to see inside Trace's mind. He would realize that Trace thought it was stupid they weren't talking, and they could just get over this little fight and move on with their lives. And then they wouldn't even have to do any actual talking about it. Trace was horrible at that kind of stuff anyway.

All right, he's got to talk to me before the day is completely over, he decided toward the middle of the last class. He and Kaos never went a full day without speaking. Even if they did get on each other's nerves. Usually, one of them would just go up to the other one and act like nothing was wrong once they had some time to get over it. This was just one of those instances, right? Maybe even Trace would go up to him after class, even if he was with Amberly, and just chat with him like nothing had happened.

But what if that makes him think I've changed my mind about the fight?

Trace hadn't changed his mind. And nothing Kaos could tell him would. He had a job now. He had to go in today at some point after school, drop off his paperwork, and get his uniform. Then, his first day would be shortly after that. This job was how he was making his money now.

Trace was conflicted as he sat at his desk. He tried to think of a plan for the remaining time of class, but when the end of the day finally came, he still didn't have a clue what to do. And based on the way Kaos quickly left, not even glancing back to look at Trace, he knew now Kaos didn't have any plans to fix things with him, either. Giving up for the time being, he walked home partway with Kire and Rose before their routes separated them. Then Trace went home, got his paperwork, and brought it back to the Montgomery

Theater. He was given his uniform, which made him even more embarrassed that he was going to be seen working here, having to wear it. After that, he was introduced to some of his new coworkers, all of whom didn't seem like any people Trace wanted to get to know or become friends with.

I'm just here for the money. I'm just here for the money. He had to keep telling himself that, or else he was afraid he would quit right there on the spot.

When he left the theater, he knew he could turn left to go back home or...

He looked to the right—it wasn't too much further to get to Kaos's fancy mansion.

Deciding he needed to tell Kaos about how Rezin came to his house impersonating him last night and that he needed to get his bike back because it was going to be his transportation to work, he walked to Kaos's house.

When he got there, he rang the doorbell and waited.

Kaos answered the door, and strangely enough, he had a smile on his face, and he looked like he just finished laughing about something.

"Hey, Trace," he said slowly, really drawing the words out as the smile slowly left.

"Hey."

The tension in the air between them was heavy. And it only grew.

"Trace?" another voice asked. Then, into the doorway stepped Amberly.

"What is this?" Trace asked, looking back and forth between the two of them. "You guys hang out together after school now?"

Suddenly, Trace wasn't finished being mad at him after all. How could he? Sure, it had annoyed Trace already that the two of them were always together at school. Yes, when all of The Unlikely Defenders were gathered together nowadays, Kaos and Amberly tended to go off and be their own pair. But seeing Amberly there, at

Kaos's house with him, also looking like she had just been laughing about something, and looking like she and Kaos were having the time of their lives without him, it struck a nerve. And Trace was furious.

"So what?" Kaos asked with a casual shrug. He didn't look the slightest bit guilty.

But Amberly did. Upon seeing Trace standing there at the door, it looked as if every ounce of remaining happiness had been drained from her. Apparently, Kaos was the only one who could make her smile.

Too upset to speak or to do much of anything else, Trace shook his head and walked back down the driveway.

"Trace!" Amberly called.

He turned around to see her running down the driveway after him. Kaos stood back still in the doorway.

"What?" Trace asked flatly.

"I... Nothing happened... Kaos and I were just hanging out."

"Uh-huh."

She opened her mouth again, but no words came out. So they just stood there staring at each other.

"Oh!" Kaos yelled from the doorway. "Don't forget your bike!"

Trace walked past Amberly up to the side of the house to grab his bike. When he turned around, Amberly hadn't left the spot she had been standing in at the bottom of the driveway.

"*Well*?" Trace asked her as he climbed on the seat. "You have anything else you want to say to me?" He didn't know what he wanted from her. Something, *anything*, to make the situation less bad. To make Trace stop feeling like his ex-girlfriend and his best friend were starting to fall for each other.

I..." Amberly trailed off.

He waited a couple seconds more, but when it became clear she didn't have anything else to say, he sped away.

All Trace wanted to do was yell. Scream. Punch something.

Kill something.

If only there was still a battle going on in the Albus realm, he thought to himself as he pedaled furiously. The thought sparked an idea in him. Maybe there weren't any battles still being held inside of the Albus realm, but he at least fit in better there with his sword. And the idea of escaping this world to go into the Albus realm sounded all too enticing.

He grabbed his sword, made his way to the portal, and went into the Albus realm through the portal. From there, he spent the next couple of hours angrily cutting and stabbing and fighting with things in the woods as he walked through it, taking his anger out on the magical forest greenery. He hardly even paid attention to where he was walking, and he completely lost his sense of time, especially since the canopy of trees created a sort of darkness that hid the sky, which was the only revealing way to tell time passing.

Eventually, he found himself inside one of the towns he had helped repair. It was bustling and full of more life and happiness than he had seen it yet. And when people started recognizing him, they flocked to him excitedly, eager to chat about his travels and what was next for his plans, as if Trace had any idea.

Not in the mood to make conversation, although he did appreciate all of the kind attention, he asked where he could get a ride to Albus's grave. And in minutes, a carriage waited for him.

When he arrived at the cemetery, slowly, Trace approached the great Albus Bridge's tombstone. He placed a hand on top of it and wished there was some way to make Albus return. They were in a magical realm, weren't they? Didn't that mean *anything* was possible?

"It's not working, Albus," Trace said, his voice quiet. "We're not united. The group might be pulling further apart than ever. I don't know if we'll ever be strong enough to defeat Rezin. I don't know what it is we need to find. I don't know what's coming. I don't know what's going to happen. And I just..." He pictured Kaos and Amberly together at his house again. "They wouldn't become a couple, right?" he asked Albus. "They wouldn't do that to me."

He waited. Maybe Albus would make a tree branch move. Maybe he'd summon some sort of magical fairy to appear out of nowhere and deliver Albus's response. Maybe Albus could somehow offer him some advice. Some way to fix all of this.

"I just don't know what to do," Trace said.

"Boy, you *really* aren't aware of your surroundings, are you?"

Trace's head snapped up, his heart nearly flying out of his chest. Emerging from the trees, not at all far away from where Trace was standing, came a redheaded girl in colorful pink and green clothing, her hair pulled back in lots of little braids.

"I've been watching you for quite some time now," she said.

"Excuse me?" Trace asked, arching an eyebrow. Who was this chick?

"The strange clothes. Your sword. Talking to one of the Albuses' graves. I heard about you. You're going around and fixing up the wreckage in all the hamlets."

"Sorry, who are you?" Trace asked, annoyed and a little embarrassed that he had been caught talking to Albus's grave. It wasn't like Albus could actually hear him. It probably looked like Trace was just talking to himself.

How lame.

The redhead before him was kind of cute, too, and it made everything worse.

"Novus Applerose," she told him. "Half-human, half-fairy. I live in one of the towns you have yet to visit. But one of my friends has written to me to tell me all about you people."

Trace looked around himself. "How long were you standing there?"

"Well... for as long as *you* have been, I suppose," she explained. "Before that, I saw your carriage stop. And I saw you get out of it. You walked through the cemetery with such determination that I wanted to know where you were going."

"Um... Oh."

She didn't even seem the least bit embarrassed about being a bit stalker-ish.

"Well, what are you doing here?" he asked.

"Visiting my mother's grave. She didn't die in the recent battle, though. Don't worry. She died a long time ago."

"I'm sorry," Trace said.

"It's all right."

She walked a little closer to him, a ray of sun shining through the trees and catching her perfectly, making her glossy red hair shimmer. Her eyes were green and sparkling. There was something a bit inhuman about her. It was as if her skin was illuminated from underneath.

"Well, just so you know, I *usually* am aware of my surroundings," Trace felt the need to say. "I've just been a bit... distracted today."

"You looked to be in great distress when you were talking to Albus. You are worried about those other heroes. My friend said the one with the fiery sword had the name Trace."

"Uh, yeah," Trace replied, not sure which question of hers he was answering or if she was even asking a question at all.

The half-human, half-fairy had an expression that was unreadable. There was a hint of a smile on her lips. A hint of mystery in her eyes. "Why is your group pulling apart?" she asked.

"Well... no offense, but I don't really know you, and it's kind of personal."

"All right. Where are the other heroes? Are they not far behind? Or did you come here alone?"

"I'm alone."

"Me too." She smiled brightly. It was so odd to see it that Trace couldn't help but chuckle.

"Okay," he said.

"If you're done talking with Albus, you should come back to my hamlet with me. The town's been eagerly waiting for your arrival. We could really use the help. Besides, my father says it's not safe for me to be walking around alone, and it might get dark soon, and it *is* sort of a long walk back."

"Oh.... sure. Okay."

How was he supposed to say no to her? He didn't like the idea of her walking around alone at night either.

"How old are you?" he asked.

"Eighteen. Just celebrated my birthday."

"Oh, happy birthday. You know, in my world, that would make you officially an adult. Is it the same here?"

"Here, our accomplishments, experiences, and knowledge all contribute to the make-up of that consideration."

"That makes sense."

As they walked alongside each other, out of the forest and over a few small hills following a dirt trail, Trace continued talking with Novus. He found her fascinating. Anything he wanted to know, she told him willingly. No matter if it was a touchy subject. She wasn't afraid to be blunt and direct. She amused him at times, too. She was a bit of a spitfire.

"I think I'd like to come to your world someday," she told him out of the blue after they just finished discussing why her favorite food was porridge and how he simply just *needed* to try some.

"Trust me, you don't," Trace told her.

"Why not?"

"People wouldn't be as accepting there of you as everyone seems to be here of us."

"Why not?"

"People in the Earth realm are just... different. Mistrusting. Judgmental. At least in Montgomery."

"Well, why would anybody want to live there then?" she asked.

"Beats me," Trace said. "I think I'd much rather live here."

"Then why don't you?"

Trace stopped walking. It took the fairy a moment to notice it, but eventually, she turned around and gave him a quizzical eyebrow raise.

"I mean... that would be impossible, wouldn't it?" Trace asked.

"I don't see how that could be true."

"Well... I have my family in the Earth realm. And time works weirdly in between the two. If I stayed here for several years and then popped back there for a visit, everyone else would still be around the same age, but I would be a lot older."

"Fascinating," she said, her eyes sparkling. She walked back over to Trace and grabbed him by the elbow to force him to resume walking with her. "Do the other heroes wish they lived here as well?"

"I don't think so," Trace mumbled. He didn't even want to talk about them. He was having too good of a time with Novus, talking about her and this world.

"We should get you some of my father's clothes," she said randomly.

Trace laughed incredulously. "What?"

"They'd look great on you. They would make you blend in well here in the Albus realm. You'd make a good fit if you wanted to stay here."

"I would?"

"Definitely. And with your sword, and your strength, and your good looks, you could be something of a knight, I'm sure. You'd get a fancy place to live. Servants. Lots of preferential treatment."

"Do you think so?"

"I do."

With the idea of it in his head now, the picture painted of the kind of life he would have here, he thought maybe it wouldn't be such a crazy thing to stay here. Maybe he could even get his mom to come here as well. They could both escape their old lives. Start fresh here.

Maybe being here would make it easier for him to get over Amberly.

23

Trace ended up having such a good time with Novus that day, just talking with her and forgetting his existence in the real world for a moment. He decided before he was taken back to the portal—via a *flying* magical carriage—that he was going to come back the next day to see her again.

It was hard for him to sleep when he got home. He just kept thinking about the Albus realm. He thought of what Nova had said about him being a good fit for living there. Could it actually be done? For some crazy reason, it felt possible. The only thing keeping him here right now was his mother. If he could take her with him, why not stay in the Albus realm?

When he finally fell asleep for the evening, he woke up the next day surprised that he had actually had good dreams. Dreams about the Albus realm. For once, Rezin hadn't been invading his sleep. He hadn't been forcing Trace and his mother to see horrible things. To relive horrible moments of their past. And it put Trace in an exceptionally good mood despite everything going on with Kaos and Amberly.

He ate a quick breakfast, greeted his mother, who surprisingly still hadn't had another drink since their fight, and left early for school because he wanted to go to the Albus realm before the day started—that was just how excited he was to get back there and back to Novus.

Novus was cute and all, but Trace wasn't interested in hanging out with her because he saw her as a potential to be something more. He genuinely liked her as a person and was happy for someone's company that didn't constantly remind him of his responsibilities or fill him with sadness because of the past they shared. But he'd be lying if he said he didn't consider it maybe being a possibility in the future for Novus and him to have a relationship.

What would it be like to date someone who was half-fairy?

The thought of actually dating her *now* made him nauseated. He still wanted Amberly back. He was still not over their breakup. And despite how it seemed that Amberly and Kaos were maybe seeing each other, Trace still loved Amberly and wasn't ready to move on.

When he finally made it into the Albus realm, he anticipated having a long walk to the hamlet where Novus resided. However, upon crossing through the glowing blue mist in the arch, he arrived on the other side to see that the magical carriage that had flown him back yesterday was still there waiting for him.

It was hard to keep track of how time worked here. Whenever they were in this world, and they came back to their own, no matter how much time they spent in the Albus realm, only a few minutes had passed in the Earth realm. But, when they *weren't* in the Earth realm, the Albus realm seemed to move in time with the Earth realm again. It was as if whoever created the two universes knew that there would be a group of individuals hopping in between the two, needing their frequent disappearances to be discreet even if they lasted a while.

The flying magical carriage was led by actual unicorns, stark white with iridescent horns on top of their heads. But these unicorns had wings. And they didn't need a carriage driver to guide them. When Trace opened the carriage door, it was completely empty, a plush purple velvet tufted cushion awaiting his bottom.

What are unicorns called again when they have wings? he wondered to himself. He was certain he had read about them or seen them in something before. He had never really been a big fantasy fiction fan, but he vaguely recalled watching *Clash of the Titans* with Kaos once.

Pegasus.

He was being flown in a magical carriage by Pegasus. In a place he never knew existed but was now considering the possibility of living in.

Amberly's words *did* replay in his head as he sat back and let the carriage lift him into the air and bring him to Novus's hamlet. Amberly had told him he didn't belong here. And maybe that was true. But who wouldn't want to live in a place like this? Who in their right mind would know that magic exists and not want to exist with it? The Earth realm seemed so boring to Trace.

He laughed and stuck his head out the window the entire carriage ride into Novus' hamlet. When the Pegasus landed on the ground sometime later, the door opened on its own, and Trace stepped out.

Novus was standing there, already waiting for him, wearing a pretty green dress that wasn't too fancy but still looked elegant, and she was smiling at him.

"That was amazing," he said, walking up to her with a grin. He had just been flying!

"I thought you might like it," she replied. "For me, it's just an everyday thing. It's somewhat amusing to see you get so excited over something so mundane here in my world. I couldn't even imagine what it would be like in *your* world."

"Trust me, don't even waste time trying to imagine it. It's not worth it. You're not missing anything," Trace assured her.

She smiled.

"So, what's the game plan for today?" he asked, eager for whatever they were going to do. He wouldn't have even minded it if she told him she wanted him to spend the day helping rebuild their hamlet. It would be easier if the others were there to help him with that, but he could at least put a little dent in the repairs without them. He was pretty dang strong, after all.

"You mean... what are we going to *do*?" Novus asked.

"Yeah." Trace thought it was amusing how, even though they spoke English, there was still somewhat of a language barrier between the two of them. Between their world and this one.

"Well..." Novus pondered aloud, "I'm trying to think of what I could show you that would be of interest to you. That would get that excited look in your eye again."

"If it involves magic, I'm going to be excited."

She let out a snicker. "Let's go for a walk, then."

"Like... a *magical* walk?"

"Sorry to disappoint; it's just a normal walk. Toward magical things, however."

They walked together through the village, and as Trace came across anyone looking like they were struggling with something, whether it be building repairs or a woman trying to get her groceries inside her house with her arms full and a toddler in tow, he would rush over to help. Everyone seemed to know who he was. Everyone was delighted to see him. They accepted his help graciously with big smiles on their faces. It made him feel good. Needed. Important.

"Everyone is glad to have you and the other Unlikely Defenders," Novus said to him as they continued their stroll out of the village and through the green, lush landscape before them. Trace wondered where it was she was going to take him.

"I'm happy to do it," Trace answered.

"It's pretty impressive. Have you... Have you actually had to fight Yash himself yet?"

Trace stopped walking. "Wait."

She turned around curiously, wondering why he did.

"What do you know about Yash?" Trace asked her.

"What do *you* know?" she asked back.

"That he is a destroyer of realms. That he has a particular hate for the *Earth* realm."

"So, you haven't come face-to-face with him," she deduced.

"Not yet."

The news made her frown. "Disappointing. I was hoping for an exciting recollection of that story. But, I suppose it hasn't happened yet."

"Yet?"

"Doesn't have to happen eventually?" Novus asked. "Isn't that your whole... purpose?"

"We are the *earth's* defenders..." he trailed off, thinking it over. "If we sealed off the portal, and Yash can't get to Earth, then I don't see why we would *need* to confront him."

"But you're also The Unlikely Defenders of the Albus realm."

"Says who?"

"Well, *aren't* you?" she asked. "You've come here. You've protected us. You've helped us rebuild after all the harm Yash's soldiers caused. You are called The Unlikely Defenders, but I don't think that chains you just to the *Earth* realm."

"I don't know if the other members of our team would agree with you."

She resumed walking, so Trace joined her.

"At least *you're* here," she said.

She's not flirting with me, is she? Trace wondered to himself. It felt strange. Still, he offered her a friendly smile. He didn't know what it was he was doing. Before the flirtation could continue, he cleared his throat. "So, what do you know about Yash?" he asked a second time.

She raised an eyebrow.

"You never told me," he pointed out.

"I've only heard stories. But I suppose the stories I've heard are probably true because why would anyone have the need to lie about anything about him? From what I heard, he's not even really...alive. A living thing. He is more of just this... entity. He looks alive. He acts alive. But he wasn't even ever 'born.' He just appeared. He is cold. Everything around him feels dead and miserable. He controls Chaos, his ship that's out there, between the planes of the universes, just floating in the black nothingness. He is a hater of hope. He thinks it's pathetic and meaningless. He controls the heat of Yarra, the living, breathing fire. That is his biggest weapon—the fire that cannot be extinguished."

Trace shuddered. A lot of this did sound familiar to him. These were the things Albus had told him once upon a time. The refresher from Novus wasn't exactly pleasant.

"And yet, a group of high schoolers are supposed to protect multiple realms from him," he said to Novus.

"What are high schoolers? That sounds fancy."

Trace laughed. "It's definitely not."

As they walked, he explained to her some things about his realm. And she was most interested to hear about it. Trace couldn't believe that she was. He would tell her the most boring fact, but it would make her gasp and widen her eyes in complete shock.

Eventually, they reached a river, the destination Novus had wanted to get them to. It was in a cluster of trees, which were hidden in the middle of some grassy plains. The further the two had walked into the trees, the darker it had gotten around them. And it wasn't because the trees created a canopy that covered the sky. There was some sort of enchantment there. Something *else* that made it perpetually dark. At all hours of the day, according to Novus.

Trace didn't understand it at first, but as soon as they reached the river, he figured it out.

The river water was *glowing*. It was as if the water itself was illuminated, not the entities inside of it. Trace had never seen anything like it. It almost looked so unnatural that he wanted to deem it unsafe to touch. To drink. To be near. It looked like the liquid he would expect to find in a vat of toxic waste. Only less viscous.

"How is it *doing* that?" Trace asked, unable to tear his eyes away. He only did when he noticed something else glowing in his peripherals, as if maybe Novus was suddenly holding up a brilliantly lit lantern.

Looking at Novus, he noticed she was glowing, too, just as brightly as the river.

"How are *you* doing that?" he gasped.

"I drank from the river," she explained. "Its effects last up to a fortnight, depending on how much you drink of it in a single sitting."

"That's..."

He couldn't stop looking at her. She was neon. Glow-in-the-dark.

"...incredible," he eventually finished.

"You should drink some," Novus suggested, smiling. Her teeth glowed, too.

"Is that all that happens? I'll become glow-in-the-dark?" he asked.

"There are some other... effects, I suppose," she admitted, a little ominously at that.

Trace stared down at the rushing river. He considered it. But after a moment, he shook his head. "I don't think I should. I have to go back to my realm. If people see me glowing in the dark, I'm going to get locked up and thrown in a lab—a very scary place in my world."

"Well, why don't you just stay until the effects wear off?"

"I..."

Trace didn't know how to explain it to her. He probably *could* stay here for multiple days, and when he arrived back in the Earth realm, only a couple of hours would have passed there. But passing the time in the Albus realm made him anxious. It made him feel as if he was missing out on things happening back in his world. He didn't think it was a good idea to stay here overnight, especially without any of the other quintets there with him.

"Maybe another time," he decided.

"Fair enough."

The two of them hung out by the glowing river for the next several hours, laughing and joking and learning more about each other. Trace sensed more flirtation coming from Novus as well, and he had a feeling she maybe had a crush on him. Especially when she found out that he and "the pretty blonde girl" weren't an item. And while Trace *was* having a nice time with Novus, it was after she discovered this about him that their conversation turned a little flirty. He was quick to become uncomfortable. He found himself thinking of Amberly.

It doesn't matter what I do, he thought to himself, trying to skip a rock into the glowing river. *I'm still always going to miss her.*

Only when Novus was hungry and exhausted, and it was well into the evening, did Trace finally walk back to her village with her and hitch a ride on the magical carriage again back to the portal.

His spirits had been high in the Albus realm, but the second he returned back to his homeland, the darkness settled over him again. This world without magic was too quick to remind him of how much he disliked it here. Of how his life was currently a mess. How things here were not at all simple.

He went home, hung out with his mother, showered, and lay in bed, dreading having to go to school tomorrow.

24

When Trace arrived on campus the next day, having ridden the bus because he refused to take a ride from Kaos, his car or any other one he was borrowing if his pretty red one hadn't been replaced yet. Trace *wanted* to refuse to see Kaos or Amberly for the whole day, but the way Kire frantically waved him down as soon as he saw him, already with all of the others, made it clear that that just wasn't going to be possible. He had a job to do regardless of whether or not he got along with the other people in their group—he couldn't put a pause on protecting the realms.

"What is it?" Trace asked in a flat voice when he reached the other Unlikely Defenders.

"Kire's been waiting for you to get here so that he can tell us all his idea at the same time," Rose pointed out.

Kire nodded, looking like he had just chugged seven espresso shots. "Are you guys totally, completely, 100 percent against... maybe... ditching school today?"

"What?" Trace asked back, noticing the shocked way Kire's girlfriend was looking at him. *So, Kire didn't even let Rose in on his idea yet?*

"I just..." Kire looked over his shoulder to make sure no one else was close enough to hear them. Then he looked back at the others. "I don't know—I was thinking we should go back to the cave."

"The cave?" Amberly asked. She looked beautiful, a vision and pink today. She should have been wearing red, though. Because in pink, she looked *way* too innocent—not at all like the *real* Amberly.

"The one where we all united for the first time and stumbled upon our gifts?" Rose asked.

"Exactly," Kire answered, smiling at her. "That was the first time there was any sort of interaction between all of us, in that spot in the cave. Sure, we've been back in the cave tons of times since then, but not at that *direct* spot. What if there's something there waiting for us? That thing Albus wanted us to have? That thing Albus needs us to have so that we can get to the bottom of this huge mess?"

Everyone stared around at each other for a moment or two. Trace was thinking it over, looking around at his other classmates beyond their group and at the school, having absolutely no desire to attend classes. School was so insignificant. Trace even thought so before he became a quintet. He didn't learn anything in school. He learned things from his real-life experiences. If it wasn't so frowned upon, he probably would've dropped out forever ago.

"I'm in," he said, shrugging.

"Same," Amberly said quickly after that, trying to catch Trace's eye. But Trace didn't want to pay her *or* Kaos any mind. There was something going on with the two of them. He wouldn't let them try to convince him otherwise.

"I... I'm pretty sure my parents will ship me off to boarding school, but okay," Rose slowly agreed.

Kaos nodded as well, not bothering to speak.

WHEN THEY FINALLY REACHED THE cave, it was Rose who led them to where they first found their gifts. The ones they found completely by accident that changed their lives forever. Rose was the one who had spent the most time in those caves before they all met. She had been working on her bioluminescence project.

"It looks so different in here," Rose said sadly as she stared around at the damp walls inside the place. "I had spent *so* much time on that project. And I completely forgot about it."

"Where did all your glowing things go?" Trace asked.

"It probably became inhabitable in here," she answered. She came to a slow stop eventually, her eyes fixed on the ground. "This is it."

Trace and Kire looked around, wondering how on earth she knew that. This part of the cave looked exactly the same as all the others.

Still, the others began searching around, too, so Trace figured he'd try. He only wished he had any idea about what it was he was supposed to be looking for.

Every time he glanced up, it seemed like Kaos was trying to move in Amberly's direction, but Amberly would move away from him as soon as she noticed it. But Trace didn't understand what the point of it was now—they had already been caught. There was no reason for Amberly and Kaos to sneak around anymore.

"What's up with you?" Rose asked, popping up beside Trace and nearly startling him.

"I'm fine," he said quickly. "Why wouldn't I be?"

"Something weird is going on with you three." She looked at him and then over at Kaos and Amberly.

"Whatever," Trace replied, trying to walk away from her.

"Okay..." Rose tried, letting out a long sigh after. "You know, this whole 'being a team' thing..."

"*I* don't need the reminding," Trace snapped, knowing he sounded bitter but unable to do anything about it. "*They* do. How can they expect me to want to be a team with them when they've both betrayed me?"

"Both of them have? You're mad at Kaos, too?"

He wished he never said anything. "Doesn't matter."

"But, what—?"

"Guys!" Amberly yelled from a few yards away. Everyone scrambled to go to where she was standing, moving a rock out of the way and pulling a medium-sized trunk out of a thick puddle of mud.

Wanting to get it out of there quicker, and *not* because he wanted to be anywhere near Amberly, Trace leaned down and helped her pluck it out.

"Do you think this is it?" Rose asked the others. "Do you think this is what Albus wanted us to find?"

"Better be," Kaos said bleakly.

Everyone stared at the trunk.

"Well... I guess one of us should open up," Kire pointed out.

They all stared at him.

"I guess *I'll* open it," he decided. Trace wasn't certain what would be waiting for them once the trunk was opened. What if some dangerous magic came out? What if it hit Trace head-on if he were to open it, and it left him horribly disfigured?

"Have at it," he told Kire, slapping him on the shoulder in a friendly, encouraging way.

Better him than me.

Kire opened the trunk. Thankfully, nothing happened. At first, Trace was worried there wasn't *anything* inside of it. But slowly, Kire took out what looked to be a tube of sorts. Inside of it, he pulled out a rolled-up piece of paper. It looked ancient.

"What's it say?" Rose asked him impatiently. Kaos walked to stand by Kire so that he could be one of the first ones to see it as Kire unrolled it. The two stood there, looking it up and down once it was opened, their eyes squinting.

"*Well*?" Amberly asked, putting a hand on her hip expectantly.

"You guys, the suspense is *killing* me!" Rose complained.

"It…" Kire trailed off and looked at Kaos. Kaos looked at him. Then he scoffed, laughed sarcastically, shook his head, and walked away from everyone.

"What?" Trace asked. "What is it?" Whatever Kaos had read, he was disappointed by it.

"Uh…" Kire handed the paper out for them to see. Amberly grabbed it, and Trace and Rose crowded around her.

Ignoring how Amberly smelled like strawberries, Trace squinted at the paper. It was a note. It wasn't signed by Albus, but Trace had a feeling it was written by him regardless.

Read closely the words inscribed upon this sacred parchment, for it reveals the path to avoid the impending doom that looms upon the Earth realm. Fate has exposed the truth once again in the form of a prophecy Yash has yet to come upon. There is only a matter of time. Within this scroll lies the truth and reason for what must come next.

Know this, young warriors: to defeat Rezin is not to end his existence. Do that, and he wins. The key to our triumph lies, instead, in his capture.

A prophecy has been unearthed by a being from the Albus realm. This prophecy remains presently veiled from Yash's watchful gaze. It holds a truth concealed from his knowing. Yet, this cover of ignorance will soon lift, and Yash shall realize the truth in its depths.

Keep clear inside your minds the revelation of this prophecy. When Yash, in his misguided arrogance, shackled his most loyal minions, Rezin, Jago, and Heno, to the Earth realm, his very own enchantments unwit-

tingly blinded him to their presence. Every form of magic, of great, great power, comes with its consequences. Those strong enough, those who believe nothing can touch them, and no one is above them, are quick to turn a blind eye to this unprejudiced truth. Yash chained living beings to a life of imprisonment. Upon doing so, his consequence was chaining himself forever to them.

Yash's command assigned three minions the solemn duty of ending the lives of those who dared impede his path. Should the first, Jago, falter, Heno was to arise, the next in line conquer and execute Yash's adversaries. And if fate should claim Heno's existence, Rezin, the third and the strongest, would step forth to fulfill what the others could not. Bound to the Earth realm, their purpose was a single quest. Ignoring that what comes with great power is great consequence, Yash unknowingly sealed his fate, becoming one with his minions' shared purpose. As the fourth alternate, should all three precursors meet their dire demise, a bridge will form, a pathway upon which Yash shall tread, seizing the opportunity to finish what his loyal minions could not. If the last of his minions is to perish, Yash will realize that the portal in the Albus realm was not his last hope of getting to the Earth realm. However, as long as Rezin lives, the bridge cannot be manifested.

"You're joking," Trace said to no one in particular, dread and anxiety filling him.

"How the heck are we supposed to do this?" Amberly complained.

"If only Rezin were a small forest critter," Rose groaned. "Then

Albus's instructions would be a piece of cake."

"It's impossible," Kaos said, irritated, still walking away from the group and shaking his head, his hands on his hips. He found a flat spot on the ground and began pacing. "We've been given an *impossible* task."

"Where would we even put him?" Amberly asked.

"Well... it has to be possible, guys," Kire said, the only one in the group who was trying to remain positive. "Or else we wouldn't be here. We wouldn't have been given those gifts in the first place. There probably wouldn't even *be* a prophecy."

"Does Halo know when Yash is going to happen upon the prophecy and learn the truth?" Trace asked Kire.

He winced. "I don't know exactly *what's* happening with Halo lately," he admits, "but the answer keeps changing. You should see it." He pauses and pulls Halo out of his backpack. He opens the up. "Look."

Trace didn't understand the point of looking inside Kire's book because he knew he couldn't understand the language Halo wrote in. Still, he walked over to see what Kire wanted him to see anyway.

The page Kire opened up to made Trace tilt his head, confused. It seemed like Halo was... *glitching*. It would write something, then it would erase it. Then, something *else* would start appearing on the page. And then that would quickly get erased, too.

"Why is Halo so uncertain?" Amberly mused allowed.

"Because the future is so uncertain," Rose commented.

"I wonder how Albus came upon the prophecy," Kire said, closing Halo back up and putting the book away. "And why he couldn't tell us about it sooner."

"Maybe he had been about to tell us," Amberly said. "You know, before... Before he died."

"Why did he have to make it so difficult for us to learn the truth?" Rose asked.

"This is obviously *very* valuable information," Kire explained. "In the wrong hands, someone could make the wrong choice."

Trace stood next to Amberly again, who was still holding the scroll up, examining it closely. He read it again as well. If Rezin died, it open up a new path for Yash to take to the Earth realm. Then he was destined to defeat those standing in his way—A.K.A., The Unlikely Defenders. And once the Defenders were out of his way, Yash's quest would be fulfilled, and he would then be free to destroy the rest of their universe as he saw fit, just like he wanted to anyway.

This was how Yash could still get to Earth. This was the other way.

25

"All right, Amberly," Kaos said as the gang stood outside of their school well after school hours in the dead of the night. "When we get inside, you go immediately to the security office, use your gauntlet thingy—"

"Gamora," Amberly corrected.

Kaos rolled his eyes. "*Gamora*—to unlock the door, turn off the cameras, and then delete the footage of us sneaking in."

Amberly nodded, lifting her arm and flexing her fingers inside of the gauntlet.

Kaos, who still had a key to the school, pulled the key out of his pocket and stuck it into the lock on the front entrance door.

"We don't have to worry about Rezin killing us if we get caught," Rose said. "Our *principal* will do that. And then so will our... guardians."

"Don't be such a baby," Amberly said, rolling her eyes.

"What is *wrong* with us?" Rose continued, ignoring her. "We spend the day avoiding school, only to come back to it when we don't even have to be here?"

"We *do* have to be here," Kaos snapped. Inside the school, he led the way to the gymnasium. The doors to it were wide open. Inside the gym, the floor was clear, and the bleachers pushed into the walls. "The gym is the perfect place to train unseen—once the cameras are taken care of, anyway."

Amberly left the group to go to the security room to destroy the footage leading up to the moment they arrived on campus. She was also going to turn off the system so that they wouldn't be recorded leaving. The security guard would come back the next day and think the system merely malfunctioned, especially since the quintets agreed to do their training without leaving any trace that they had ever been there at all.

Meanwhile, the others spread out on the floor of the gymnasium, ready to go with their gifts. Kaos had called this meeting with everyone. He thought they all needed to start group training immediately. He still thought it was an impossible task to *capture* Rezin instead of kill him—even killing him was proving to be extremely difficult—but he pointed out that if the group had any chance at all of succeeding, they needed to be at their strongest, and they needed carefully, meticulously devise the best possible plan of attack.

"Just merely getting together and practicing with our gifts isn't what is going to make us stronger as a team," Rose reminded everyone, looking back and forth between Trace and Kaos, the two who were fighting. Then, when Amberly returned to the room, Rose shot her a look, too.

"Yeah, speaking of that," Kaos said as Amberly joined their circle, nodding at everyone to tell them the security footage was all taken care of, "whatever ridiculous, insignificant drama going on among each other in the group, we need to push it aside and forget about it. I don't care about any of your problems. I don't care about whatever issues you guys have. Me? I'm good. *I* don't have a problem with any one of you. You all need to get on the same page as me."

Kaos wouldn't even look at Trace though as he spoke, which made Trace certain Kaos was *full* of it. He rolled his eyes and clenched his jaw.

"It's easier said than done," Amberly mumbled, getting on the ground and stretching as if she was about to begin cheerleading practice.

"Okay, *wise leader*," Kire said, changing the subject abruptly. "Do you even have any idea as to *how* we're going to capture Rezin? Capture him and not kill him? And without letting *him* kill *us*?"

"Not a clue," Kaos admitted quickly. "But, hey—you're a smart guy, Kire. Figure something out for us, will you?"

"You're not putting that on me!" Kire barked.

"We can brainstorm *together*," Rose said, acting as the group's mediator.

"For now, we need to see where we're at with our compatibility as a team. How strong we are with our gifts," Kaos said, straightening his crown. "Let's run some drills."

The gang practiced together. Rose had brought in some strands of grass from outside before they entered, so she opened her palm and started manipulating and making them grow, turning them into something much bigger.

Amberly pulled a punching bag out of the supply closet and threw an intense punch at it, sending it across the room. Then, she would use her ability to lift the punching bag and bring it soaring back across the gym toward her.

Kire was working with Halo, writing something inside of it and muttering something under his breath, like he was maybe trying to get the book to stop freaking out. Or maybe he was trying to work out ways he could make it produce a bigger shield.

Kaos concentrated on trying to hear inside the minds of people outside the school, as far away as he could reach them.

Trace worked on his sword-fighting skills, not wanting to do too much with the fire in case he accidentally destroyed the school. They had to be careful not to make any messes because they didn't have Albus anymore to clean up after them.

"Yeah—this isn't working," Kire said after a while, getting to his feet and closing Halo. Trace was in complete agreement. The fire engulfing his sword and cascading up his arm was weak.

"Yeah. I'm already exhausted," Amberly said, out of breath. Then she pointed at Rose. "And her nose is bleeding."

Worried, Kire ran over to Rose, who turned away from everyone and wiped her nose on her sleeve. "I'm fine. Just a little dizzy."

"What did I tell you guys?!" Kaos snapped. "We need to be unified!"

"We know that, Kaos," Amberly said. "I'm trying, I just…" She looked at Trace.

"I don't know," Trace said. "Maybe there'd be a better chance of getting Rezin captured if we handed our gifts off to another group of people. One much more likely to get along with each other. The lunch ladies all seem to be pretty close."

"Don't be so negative," Rose said to him, ignoring his joke. "Instead of practicing with our gifts, weakening ourselves even further because we're clearly *not* united, we need to probably just work out our problems—have a nice group therapy session."

"Ew," Amberly said.

"Absolutely not," Kaos added.

Trace stayed silent.

Rose groaned. "We're doomed," she said. "Simply doomed. We might as well start preparing Yash's welcome party."

26

Trace shook his head at Kire when Kire approached him at the snack kiosk inside the old movie theater—Trace's new place of employment.

"Here for your free tickets?" Trace asked him from behind the counter, knowing it was only going to be a matter of time before one of his friends came in here to visit him.

"I'll take some free popcorn," Kire said, "but I'm not here to see a movie."

"You can't stand around and bug me," Trace said, looking around for his manager to make sure he wasn't spotted slacking off, hanging out with Kire. Luckily, he couldn't see his manager anywhere.

"I'm not," Kire said. "I just want some popcorn."

"No one comes to the movie theater *just* to get popcorn and not to go see a movie," Trace said, not buying a word of it. Still, he grabbed a bag of popcorn, the small size because he wasn't sure how much free popcorn he was allowed to give away—and reached over the counter to give it to Kire.

"Oh, *awesome!*" Kire dove into the popcorn, but he didn't leave the kiosk. No one else was in line to order a snack or drink because, currently, in both theaters, the movies had already started. There wouldn't be another rush of customers until those movies ended and the new ones were about to start.

"What do you want?" Trace asked, trying to look busy by pretending to sweep behind the counter. He had already done this four times today; there was nothing left to sweep.

"Yesterday didn't go well," Kire said.

"Yeah, no duh." Trace knew Kire was referring to the time they had all spent trying to "be a team" inside the school gym last night.

"There's only really been... I think... once?" Kire continued, the statement sounding like a question.

"Once what?" Trace asked.

"There has only been one time where we all kicked butt because we were all in sync. Because we all trusted each other and wanted the same things," Kire explained, keeping his voice low, leaning in closer to Trace.

Trace sighed and tucked the broom away. He rested his palms on the counter and glared at him. "You don't understand," he told Kire, "I'm pretty sure *you'd* be pretty annoyed, too, if you and Rose broke up and you came over to my house to see the two of us hanging out together without you."

"*Oh,*" Kire said, finally realizing the situation between Trace, Amberly, and Kaos.

"I just... I *know* something is going on between them, dude," Trace continued.

"What do you mean, you *know*? Like, you *saw* it happen for a fact? Did they kiss or something in front of you?"

"No. But I wouldn't be surprised if they have kissed." The thought made him feel sick. "You've seen them—they never leave each other alone!"

"Well, yeah... but because they're friends."

When Kire saw the way Trace glared at him, he raised up his hands in surrender and then ate some more popcorn.

"I'm not saying you're wrong," Kire continued. "I'm just trying to give some other possible explanations. If you want, I can try and find out if there is, *for a fact*, something going on between the two of them. My sister loves me now, you know."

"Yeah, *right*." It was weird to hear Kire even referring to Amberly as his sister.

"It's true. We've gotten past our issues. Rose and I are doing really well, too. All that is holding the team up is you guys. So, you gotta get past it."

"Yeah. Well... I know you're right, dude, but it's not exactly simple."

"Make it simple."

Trace grabbed a towel and started wiping things down. "Hey, what's going on with your dad, anyway?"

"What about him?"

"Just... With Amberly. With the money. That whole situation. You don't have to talk about it if you don't want to."

"It's... Well... Let's just say there's a reason I am wandering around this movie theater instead of hanging out back at my place. I don't know what's going on with my parents. I don't know what's going to happen. But my mom is making my dad continue to give money to Amberly. So at least there's something good coming out of all of it."

"Do you think they'll get divorced?" Trace asked.

Kire shrugged. "I don't know. I think my mom hates him. But divorcing isn't apparently simple. Not when it comes to dividing everything up and setting Mom up to be able to live sufficiently without him. and then there's custody of me... I sort of think they're just waiting until I'm eighteen. I think I'm just going to keep yelling at each other until then."

"Yikes. That's rough."

Kire shrugged. "In all honesty, I can actually say I'm glad this whole situation with Amberly happened. For years, I wanted some-thing to happen that finally convinced my mom that my dad is a horrible monster that she should stay far away from. And I think finding out he's had a child for all these years that he never helped care for might finally have been the thing to push her over the edge."

"Huh," Trace mused. "And... how is Amberly doing with all of it? Is your mom forcing Gerald to talk to her or spend time with her, too?"

Kire shrugged. "No. They haven't spoken. I am still the gopher, delivering the goods every week. But it's okay. Amberly seems completely fine with how it's all worked out. She doesn't expect anything else. Just what she deserves."

Trace laughed because he couldn't believe what he was hearing out of Kire's mouth. "Kire Hunter complimenting Amberly McHenry. Now I *know* this realm is completely ruined."

Kire rolled his eyes and started walking away. "Fix it, dude," he called over his shoulder to Trace. "Before Halo stops glitching and finally comes up with a concrete answer about the future of our existence. Because I have a feeling when that happens, it's going to mean that it's coming really soon."

27

When Trace got home from work that night, he walked inside his house and noticed that his mother wasn't in her usual spot on the couch in front of the TV. He wasn't worried. He did find it strange, but he was curious. He couldn't see any empty bottles of alcohol strewn about. That was a good sign. And maybe the fact that she wasn't sitting on the couch was another good sign. Maybe she was off doing something productive.

He sniffed the air, but he didn't smell any dinner being cooked.

"Mom?" he called, wondering if she was even there at all. He didn't get a response from her. He slowly walked through the house, looking for her. Room after room, he searched, calling for her and growing increasingly concerned when she didn't call back, even as he grew nearer to her bedroom.

"Mom, are you home?"

She never went anywhere. She always had her groceries delivered to the house. She wasn't the type who liked to continuously get her hair and nails done. And if she were going to go somewhere, she would have either left a note or given Trace a call.

Standing just inside of her bedroom, Trace finally heard something.

"I'm in here!"

Trace could barely hear her voice. He realized it was because it was coming from inside of her walk-in closet, inside her bathroom.

He followed the voice. Inside the large walk-in, Vivian was sitting there on the floor, her arms around her knees.

Disappointment immediately swam through Trace's veins. Her being so out of place like that, hiding out somewhere so ridiculous, it could've only meant one thing.

His mother was drinking again.

"Mom, get up," he snapped, reaching down to grab her hand and pull her to her feet.

"I'm so glad you're finally home," she said.

He ignored her. "Where are you hiding all the bottles now, huh?"

"What?" she asked, looking stunned. "No, Trace, that's not—"

"You know what, Mom? You know what it's taken for me to get the money for your medication? The kinds of things I've done?"

"Trace, you're not—"

He interrupted her again.

"I've done *bad* things, Mom. Bad things to get you the money for your pills. Bad things, just for you to use the money for your alcoholic ways instead. I put my future in jeopardy just for you to waste yours."

"What are you talking about?" she whispered, looking deeply offended.

"I have been street fighting! For money! I even robbed a corner store!"

"You... you didn't," she stammered. "You wouldn't do that. Not my boy."

"I did! Because you pushed me that far! Because I had no other options!"

"But you... you have a job. You..."

"I have a job *now*! I didn't before. Did you really never wonder how I was getting the cash? You never asked. Don't get mad at me now, Mom. I always thought you didn't care how I got the money as long as I got it."

"Just stop!" she cried. "Please!" She grabbed onto Trace and shook him slightly. "Stop with all of this and just listen to me for *one* second!"

"Why should I?!"

"Because I'm *not* drunk!"

He tried to pull out of her grasp, but she only held on tighter.

"Look at me!" she demanded. "I'm speaking clearly. I'm not swaying. My breath doesn't smell like alcohol. I'm telling you the truth."

Trace hadn't even considered these points. But... his mom was right. She wasn't showing any of her usual symptoms of drinking.

"But... What are you—why were you just sitting in here like this then?"

"Well, I was *trying* to tell you until you started yelling at me!"

"Mom, what happened?"

"I've been hiding in here. Waiting for you to get home. I was just too scared to even leave the closet to go get my phone and call you."

"Hiding?" Trace's stomach lurched. "From what?"

"From *who*," she corrected. "Your father, that's who!"

There's no way I heard her correctly, Trace thought, his lips parting in complete shock and disbelief.

"What did you just say?" he asked, his voice barely audible.

"He was here! You don't have any idea how much power it took to just step away from the door and not answer it," she told him. "There were so many things I wanted to say to him. After all these years... But I didn't do it, Trace. Because I knew it wouldn't be good for any of us. He kept knocking. He kept saying he just wanted to talk. I don't know how he knew I was home because even when I didn't answer, he didn't give up. Oh, Trace, it was *horrible*." Her eyes filled with tears. "He started walking around the perimeter of the house, trying to stare through all of the windows. That's why I came into the closet. I felt like it was the only place he couldn't see me. *You* didn't see anyone out there, did you?"

"Why would he come here?" Trace asked. "Why now? After all of these years?"

She shook her head. "I don't know. But Trace, if I had still been drinking, I would've answered the door." She coughed weekly. She looked a little unsteady on her feet.

"Let's go sit you down," Trace said, trying to remember if he saw anyone creeping near the house before he went inside. It was dark out, and he hadn't been paying that much attention.

"When did this happen?" Trace asked.

"I... I don't remember."

"Mom, how long were you hiding in the closet?"

"Let's just say it was still daylight out."

"I'm so sorry," he said, feeling bad about his stupid movie theater job. If he didn't have the job, he would've been here so much sooner.

"That's all right, Trace. How could you have known he would just show up like this? Out of the blue, probably bored and just trying to ruin our lives?"

Her words struck a chord inside Trace. "Mom, how did you know it was Dad?" he asked, helping Vivian onto the sofa and making sure the curtains were closed.

"When he first knocked, I walked over to the peephole. I assumed it was a solicitor."

Trace nodded. "So, you saw him?"

"Yes. I promise you, it was your father, Trace. I know it's been a while, but it was him."

"Yeah, I believe you about that. I just... I have to ask you something weird."

She waited.

Trace's heart was racing. "Mom, was he wearing sunglasses?"

"Yes," she said in a confused tone. "Why?"

Trace's dad hadn't *really* come back—it was Rezin, thinking he'd mess with Trace's mother while he wasn't home. It was only Rezin wanting to hurt the people Trace cared about most. And Rezin knew just how to do it.

"Mom, you're home alone for too long during the day. Too often. I have school and work and soccer, stuff with my friends... I can't always come straight home to you. And when Rez—*Dad* comes back around, he could actually break in next time. Or worse."

"I was worried you were going to say something like that."

"You know I'm right. I think... I think you need to get a job, Mom. You need to get out of this house. We need to save up all the money we can so we can get out of here someday. Somewhere Dad can never find us."

She sighed. "Well... I *have* felt leaps and bounds better since I stopped drinking, even if it was rough at first. And I have to admit, getting out of here? I really do like the sound of that."

And I like the idea of making sure Rezin can never come near you ever again.

28

The moon glowed over the quiet neighborhood as Trace approached Amberly's new house, where she resided with her aunt after her mother passed. Each step felt slow and heavy as he prepared himself for what was about to happen.

When he reached the front door and rapped his knuckles against the weathered wood, it was Amberly who swung open the door. Her eyes instantly filled with fury and pain.

"What do you want, Trace?" she spat, her voice laced with bitterness.

Trace took a deep breath, trying to find the courage to say what he came here to. "We need to talk, Amberly," he started, his voice steady despite emotions raging inside him. "We need to really talk. About how things ended. About everything that happened after it did."

Amberly crossed her arms, her blue eyes still cold. She was in a fluffy robe. She had taken all of her makeup off for the night. Trace was one of the few people in the world Amberly didn't mind seeing her bare face. "Why bother? I don't owe you anything. Especially not after the way you just... abandoned me like you did."

A flash of anger surged through Trace. "*Abandoned*? When? What are you even talking about?"

Shouldn't she be trying to explain to him why she was hanging around his best friend so much lately?

"When my mom died, you jerk-wad!"

"Wh—yo—I—*you're* the one who shut *me* out, Amberly! You pushed me away and refused to let me in. How was I supposed to know how to help you when you built a fortress around yourself and made it seem like you didn't want me near you?"

Amberly's eyes narrowed. "Oh, so it's my fault?" she asked, her voice dripping with sarcasm. "I didn't realize. Sorry I couldn't act the way you wanted me to when I was dealing with the grief of losing the only parent in my life!"

Trace's fists clenched. She wasn't understanding him. She wasn't being fair. He wasn't the only one who messed this up. "Well, you...you're the one who went and betrayed me after it happened!"

"Betrayed? You think I *betrayed* you? How?! You betrayed me! You weren't there, and I really—" She cut herself off abruptly.

"You tried to end your life. You ignored me for days before that. You made it clear that I always cared about you a heck of a lot more than you ever cared about me. And then, after we broke up, what did you do?"

She opened her mouth, but no words came out.

Trace answered for her. "You ran into *Kaos's* arms. Apparently, it was okay for him to comfort you. My best friend. While I was left in the dark, wondering when I suddenly became not good enough."

Amberly's face flushed with her anger. "You're so *blind*, Trace! I didn't run to Kaos. He was there for me when you weren't! He listened, he cared, while you were too busy pretending like I didn't even exist."

How do we get past all of this resentment? How can I make her see that I never meant to hurt her? That I had thought I was doing the right thing by giving her space? I thought that was what she needed. Kaos told me she did!

"I never stopped caring, Amberly. But you pushed me away without giving me a chance to understand. I deserved more than being cast aside for my best friend."

Amberly's face twisted up. Trace could see her trembling. "You didn't even try to fight for us, Trace. When things got tough, you took the easy way out. You only thought about yourself."

Trace's stubbornness grew. "Don't pretend like you didn't have a hand in tearing us apart. You pushed me away, and I couldn't keep chasing after you when I didn't think you wanted me to."

"Keep chasing me?" she asked. "Kaos told me you were avoiding me on purpose because you didn't want to deal with me pouting!"

Silence descended upon them.

"Amberly, did you really believe that?" Trace finally asked, his voice cracking. "You believed I didn't want to *deal* with you?"

She was silent.

Trace shook his head. "I don't think I am the one who is blind here. Or, wait—are you even telling me the truth right now? Or are you trying to come up with a good excuse for how you were so quick to move on with Kaos?" The fact that she still hadn't denied her involvement with him was driving him crazy.

"You think I just moved on?" Amberly's eyes filled with tears. "I didn't move on, Trace. I'm not with Kaos."

Finally.

Relief flooded him. It filled him with immediate warmth. The good kind of heat. It dissipated some of his anger. He believed her. He had just needed her to say it.

"I... I think I see what's really going on here," he finally said.

"Wh-what do you mean?" Amberly asked, sniffling.

"Kaos told you the lie about me not wanting to be around you. And he told me the lie about how you just wanted space."

Her lips parted with the realization.

Someone else had betrayed Trace—it wasn't the girl standing there before him. It was his best friend.

Trace and Amberly stood there, silently staring at each other.

Who was going to be next to speak? What was going to happen?

Amberly took a step toward him, uncrossing her arms. She looked as if she was about to say something. Trace was dying to hear it. But before she could, her phone buzzed, interrupting them.

Amberly answered the call, her eyes still locked with Trace's. "What is it, Kire?"

Trace's frustration resurfaced, the interruption testing his patience. "Amberly, what's going on? What does he want?"

Amberly's gaze flickered between the phone and Trace, a glimmer of anticipation dancing in her eyes.

"Okay," she said into the phone with a sigh, nodding. "You don't have to—he's with me. We... we're coming." She said goodbye to Kire and hung up.

"What's going on?" Trace asked again, worried.

"Kire just told me Halo confessed something. Something that could solve our problems."

Trace's frustration evaporated. "About Rezin?"

Amberly nodded. "We should... go meet him and the others."

Trace nodded. "Yeah." The rest of their conversation was going to have to wait.

29

In the dimly lit back room of Aunt Marg's, Trace, Amberly, Rose, Kaos, and Kire gathered around a cloth-covered wooden table. Everyone was anxious to hear what Kire had to say about Halo's revelation. There was tension in the air, too, between Kaos, Trace, and Amberly. Still. Trace was able to put his anger toward his best friend to the side because he knew this was more important. The quintets had faced many challenges together before, but Rezin was the only one to prevent them from figuring out how to defeat him. They had yet to come up with a plan that worked. So, whatever Halo had to them, Trace hoped desperately she had the answer they had all been searching for.

Kire's voice was urgent as he addressed the group. "Listen, guys —we've been approaching this the wrong way."

"Is that what Halo told you?" Kaos asked. Trace wondered if he was oblivious to the fact that he and Amberly just figured out about his betrayal.

"Yeah. Listen," Kire snipped. "Our individual powers alone aren't enough to capture Rezin. We need to tap into the full potential of the Albus realm."

Amberly's gaze met Kire's, her expression confused and doubtful. "What do you mean? How can the Albus realm help us? Rezin can't go there."

Kire's eyes sparkled. "I know, but the Albus realm is a source of ancient wisdom and powerful artifacts, isn't it? If we can find the right objects, if we ask for help, we can harness their power and capture Rezin. We have access to a realm filled with... untapped potential!"

Trace's mind raced, contemplating the possibilities. The idea of combining their strengths with the vast resources of the Albus realm gave him hope. It had been a while since he had any of that. "So, what's the plan?" he asked, leaning forward with interest.

KIRE LEANED IN, too. "Halo mentioned we should seek help to find special items that will help us capture him."

The group exchanged glances. Then they discussed the next steps, and without hesitation from any of them, they rose from the table. Trace's heart was pounding. It was time for The Unlikely Defenders to embark on another quest.

His gaze met Amberly's, and their eyes reflected understanding.

They were united.

THE ALBUS REALM waited for Trace and the others, the land's wonder and enchantment unfurling around them. Trace had been quick to lead the way to the half-ruined, once serene hamlet where Novus resided.

"So, who is it you know here?" Amberly asked, clearing her throat.

Trace didn't have time to explain. He approached the nearest villager and asked where Novus's cottage was. The stranger kindly pointed in the direction they needed to go, thanking the five of them for everything they had done to protect their world.

Approaching the cottage a short while later, Trace's heart quickened with a mix of excitement and uncertainty. He couldn't ignore Novus's growing interest in him, and he was unsure whether or not Amberly would catch on to it. And what she would do if she did.

Novus opened the door and smiled. It was daylight in the Albus realm, but even still, her half-fairy heritage sprang a captivating presence. "Trace, hi," she chimed melodiously. "What brings you and your friends here?"

Stepping forward, Trace locked eyes with Novus, trying to show his urgency. "I am hoping you can maybe help us, Novus. We're on a... quest. A quest to capture one of Yash's minions who lives in our realm. I was hoping you might know of any magical artifacts that could help us."

A mischievous glimmer danced in Novus's eyes, and she nodded. "Ah, I definitely do. Which one do you want? The Veil of Binding, The Exiler, or perhaps The Prism of Shadows? There are many others, but I have found *those* ones to be the most useful when it comes to... apprehending a bandit."

The gang looked at each other briefly.

"Here, come in," Novus said. "We shouldn't discuss this out here in the open."

Everyone entered the small, quaint cottage.

"Trace, are you going to introduce me?" Novus asked.

Trace blushed and did as requested, trying to be quick about it and get back on topic before anyone could ask questions. "So, uh, these things you mentioned. What do they do?"

Novus smiled around at everyone. "It's lovely to meet you all. Trace and I have been spending time together lately, and I believe we are becoming good friends. I bet I will become good friends with each of you as well."

"Sorry, *how* did you and Trace meet?" Amberly asked her, sounding fake-nice.

"Not now," Trace muttered under his breath, shooting Amberly a look before turning back to Novus. "The artifacts," he tried again.

Novus nodded. "Right. Each possesses unique properties that can surely assist in your pursuit."

Amberly's expression tightened subtly. "And where might we find these artifacts, Nyla?"

"It's Novus," Rose corrected. Trace was certain Amberly remembered this already, though.

Novus's smile remained radiant, yet a trace of unease crossed her expression. "They're all at The Raven Botanica."

"What is that?" Rose asked, her face lighting up with her intrigue.

Novus looked stunned. "You haven't been to The Raven Botanica yet?"

They all shook their heads.

Novus turned away from them and opened a cupboard in the cozy living area. It was overflowing with various objects, and it was very disorganized. She talked to them while rummaging around for something. "Oh, you're going to love it. It has every magical item you could ever hope to have!"

"That sounds perfect," Kire said.

"And how do we obtain these objects once we get there? I assume they're not free."

Novus chuckled, still searching through the cupboard. "Most definitely not."

"But... we don't have any of this realm's currency," Amberly pointed out.

Trace doubted they had a bank where they could convert their dollars into whatever they called the money here.

Finally, Novus cried out, "Got ya!" when she found the thing she had been wanting. She turned to the others, holding a folded piece of very old paper out to them. "You'll be needing this to find the place."

Trace, being closest, took the map from her, giving her a friendly smile and pretending to be oblivious to the way she flirtatiously looked up at him from underneath her lashes. "Thanks," he told her.

Novus sighed gently and straightened up. "As for money, I happen to have some here you could borrow."

"We can't just... accept your money," Kire said, shaking his head quickly.

"We don't know how or when we would be able to pay you back," Rose added.

Novus shrugged. "How about a trade, then?"

Trace grew nervous, wondering what she would want to trade for.

"Depends," Amberly answered.

"On?" Novus asked.

"On what you want."

"Amberly," Kire said, "I don't think we have room to bargain. Do you have any other ideas for how we can get the money to buy those things Novus mentioned?"

She clenched her jaw tightly and crossed her arms instead of answering him.

"Exactly," Kire said before turning back to Novus. "What would you like?"

She tapped a finger to her chin. Trace avoided her gaze, but he could tell she had glanced at him. "How about this. I will give you the money if you promise to do me a favor in the future whenever I am in need of it."

"What favor?" Amberly asked.

"I don't know yet."

"Then how can we—?" she started to argue, but Kaos nudged her into silence.

"We'll do you one favor," Kaos said, "in exchange for the money for those goods. Whatever time you'd like, whatever favor you want, as long as it's within reason."

Novus bounced on her toes, grinning. "Deal." She held her hand out to Trace, wanting him to shake on it. But, being the group's leader, Kaos was the one who reached out and sealed the deal.

Novus disappeared into her bedroom, and when she returned, she had a small velvet pouch in her hand. "This should be more than enough."

"I don't have a good feeling about this," Amberly muttered under her breath. Only Trace and Kire were close enough to hear her.

Kaos took the pouch and nodded. "We better get moving," he told the gang.

"Thank you, Novus," Rose said. "You have no idea how much your help means to us. I like your dress, by the way."

Novus beamed at her. "My mother made it."

Feeling overwhelmingly grateful to have made a friend in Novus, Trace and his companions bid farewell to her.

30

And so The Unlikely Defenders made their way deeper into the Albus realm, toward their destination: The Raven Botanica. It was a beautiful place, created out of the ruins of what used to be a castle. The map from Novus led them there with ease, and the journey only took a few hours. Once they stood before it, staring at everything before them, at everyone crowding the place, doing their shopping and chatting with each other leisurely. It reminded Trace of a supercenter back in the Earth realm, only this one was nicer to look at and full of magical artifacts, potion ingredients, and other procurements.

The group exchanged excited glances.

"We're here for three things and three things only," Kaos instructed. "Don't get too side-tracked."

"Why not?" Rose asked, giving him a dirty look. "It's not like we're losing much time back home."

"We don't know when Rezin is going to attack next. Every second counts."

Rose rolled her eyes. Trace walked ahead of them, not wanting to be near Kaos a second longer.

I'll browse as long as I want. Kaos couldn't boss him around. It was strange to him how different Kaos looked now. Trace no longer recognized him.

He's no friend of mine.

The others wasted no time, just as Kaos wanted. They all wandered through the emporium, their eyes peeled for the objects they needed as everyone around them kept shooting curious stares.

Kire located The Prism of Shadows. It was small and cylindrical. Trace wondered how he even came across it among so much stuff.

Amberly found the Veil of Binding. She hadn't even been looking for it; she claimed she went to try on a pretty silk robe, and it was hanging right next to it. The veil didn't look like much. It was long, needing to be folded several times to not drape on the floor. It looked like basic white mesh fabric. It was wild to Trace that it contained magic at all.

Trace found The Exiler. It was a small brown metal cage that fit in the palm of his hand, with a very small lock on it. It looked like a cage for a beetle. But apparently, according to one of the shop workers, once it was unlocked, it sucked the object aimed at it right inside, containing them in a world of nothingness. Trace found it by all the other "Magical Traps".

Novus had been right when she said she gave them more than enough coins to pay for it all. They still had a few left over after. They walked outside, all hunched together to look over the objects together.

"Ah, young seekers of knowledge," a voice said as a shadow fell over them.

Looking up, Trace saw it was Albus, the still-alive one the gang knew from previous trips to this realm. With his long flowing robes and beard graying with wisdom, he appeared seemingly out of nowhere, like he just glided right out of the trunk of the tree behind him.

Trace stepped forward. "Albus, how'd you know we'd be here?"

"I've been keeping my eye on you. Seeking some aids for your quest, are we now?"

"Yes," Kaos said, puffing his chest out bravely, holding the veil in his arms.

"We think they'll help us capture Rezin," Kire added. "We found a note from *our* Albus. We have to capture Rezin. Not kill him."

Albus's eyes twinkled. "Ah, the fate of worlds lies upon your shoulders once again. How admirable."

"Any tips?" Rose squeaked.

"Remember, young friends, seekers of justice, that the path to power is often treacherous. Stay true to your purpose. *And* to one another." His voice was deep and booming, and it resonated deep within Trace's soul.

They all nodded solemnly as Albus continued. "But heed my warning, Defenders. Darkness still lurks within the heart of your companion, Kaos. It festers and grows. He has the power to stop the spread of it. But there is a challenge that comes with getting him to want to. So, beware, for it poses a peril that may surpass even the malevolent Rezin."

Everyone looked directly at Kaos, who glared at the wizard.

I don't doubt it at all, Trace thought.

Albus then locked eyes with each of them in turn, even Kaos himself. "Do not underestimate the power of this darkness. Stay vigilant, for it is during times of great turmoil that one's true nature is revealed. As for the rest of you, you are all growing in the right direction. Keep on that path. Help each other not to stray."

"You don't know what you're talking about," Kaos said to him.

Albus merely stared at him. Then, slowly, he turned to leave them. "Farewell, Defenders. And good luck."

He entered The Raven Botanica, and not knowing what to say, they all walked on.

"Should we go back to our realm now?" Kire asked.

"We should return the rest of the coins to Novus," Trace said.

"She never said we had to," Amberly pointed out. Trace offered her a smile. "Yeah, but if we go back to her place, she might let us take her Pegasus back to the portal."

"Pegasus?" Amberly asked, seeming to consider it.

"Oh my God, we *have* to!" Rose cried. Apparently, the fantastical creature was one of the few animals she wasn't terrified of.

"I wouldn't mind checking it out, too," Kire said. Kaos said nothing. He was standing off to the side, glowering.

Kire held the stone out. Now that they knew where Novus's cottage was, they could add her location to the list of places the stone could take them.

With Albus's words etched in his mind, Trace refused to take his eyes off Kaos as they circled around the stone and prepared to go through the dizzying experience of teleporting. How could any of them trust Kaos now? How could they be sure he still wanted the same things as the rest of them?

He supposed the only thing he could do about it was wait and see.

As the Pegasus-led carriage they were borrowing for the journey back to the portal—thanks to Novus—soared through the skies, Trace watched the landscape beneath him. The wind whipped through his hair and tried to force his eyes closed. He was exhausted. They all were. But it didn't matter. There was hardly any time for rest. Even now.

Around him, his friends admired the breathtaking view, their eyes wide with awe and excitement. Kire leaned forward, looking more awake than any of them. "I can't believe we're actually flying! This is incredible!"

Rose's giggled and squeezed his forearm. "Yeah, it's like a dream come true. I've always wanted to see a Pegasus."

Amberly grinned, too. "This beats any roller coaster ride, that's for sure."

Kaos observed the land below in silence. He was an outcast. Albus's words had exiled him.

The rest of the quintets' chatter filled the carriage. They were all happy to be distracted from what was coming by the ride through the sky. Trace looked at the veil in Kaos's arms and thought about Novus, the one who made them able to retrieve it. What would her favor be? She seemed so quick to believe they'd fulfill her future favor in exchange for her money. It seemed all of The Unlikely Defenders were well-trusted in the Albus realm. Trace was grateful for it, but he also worried, as he side-eyed Kaos, if they were maybe all a little *too* trusting.

And what if *they* had been too trusting of Novus?

Since he wasn't going to get any sleep, Trace leaned forward, ready to discuss what was next. "So, when Rezin strikes again, how is this going to go down?"

Kire was quick to answer. "You're going to light a circle of fire with your sword. We'll toss the prism inside the ring, and it should strip Rezin of his fighting abilities."

Amberly nodded, her eyes gleaming with confidence. "And that's when we'll throw the Veil of Binding over him, which supposedly will prevent him from teleporting or turning invisible."

"And once the fiery circle is extinguished, Amberly will use her gauntlet to manipulate any nearby water and extinguish any flames left from Trace's fire," Kire said.

Kaos watched them all from the corner seat in the carriage. He said nothing. He was too busy still moping over what Albus had warned.

"And then we'll seal him away in The Exiler, a pocket dimension where he'll be trapped between all realms, unable to escape," Rose finished.

As the carriage descended, the portal to the earth waited for them. They all climbed out, their adrenaline and confidence fading slightly. It was one thing to *talk* about the plan. Actually executing it was going to be the most difficult thing they'd ever done.

31

As they walked through the dimly lit cave, Trace found himself staring at Amberly. Back in the Albus realm, he and Amberly had hardly had any time alone to finish their talk. Trace wanted to be sure to do that with her before he did anything about Kaos, though. Trace wanted nothing more than to call Kaos out, to make him admit it was his fault Trace and Amberly broke up in the first place. But he didn't want to risk upsetting Amberly.

Amberly caught Trace eyeing her. She blushed and tucked some hair behind her ear.

Kaos is the reason I was separated from you for so long.

Trace knew he had to get better at communicating with Amberly. He never wanted to find himself in a situation like this with her again.

The large open cavern echoed with the sound of their footsteps as the group emerged from the dark tunnels. The moment they stepped into the open space, Trace froze, and his eyes widened.

Rezin.

He stood before them, his dark presence radiating malice.

Inside, Trace began to panic. He thought they'd have more time than this. He didn't think Rezin would ambush them when their plan to capture him hadn't even gotten the chance to become engrained into any of their memories!

Amberly was the first to step forward, her gauntlet shimmering with magical energy. Trace was stunned. "We're not underestimating you this time, Rezin. We've come prepared."

Halo floated in the air beside Kire, the pages flipping rapidly as it emitted a protective shield around the group before any of them had even asked for it to be conjured. The fact that Halo had taken precautionary measures only made him more alarmed.

Kaos smirked at Rezin, his crown glinting ominously. "And don't worry, Rezin. I'll make *sure* you cooperate."

With a bellowing roar, Rezin unleashed his powers. Illusions danced before Trace's eyes. Scenes switched frantically, like a skipping DVD. He saw his father hitting his mother. Then, Kaos kissing Amberly right in front of him. He saw his mom on a hospital bed, skin and bone and close to death.

Between it all, Rezin hurled his balls of energy, aiming for the vulnerable spots within the group.

Trace yelled loudly, swinging his flaming sword and creating fiery arches that lit up the cavern. "Stay focused! Remember our plan!"

If only I could get my flames to make a ring around Rezin!

The visions were making it hard for him to see clearly. To think properly. He caught a glimpse of the real world, where Amberly dodged a ball of energy, her gauntlet glowing as she launched a telekinetic punch that sent Rezin reeling.

"Yes, Amberly!" Trace shouted. Amberly turned in his direction, but then she began screaming. Rezin was making her see something. Something awful.

"No," Trace whispered, moving to shake her out of it. Before he could get anywhere close to her, he was lifted off his feet, soaring through the air in his living room. His dad cackled in the background as he flew into the wall, hitting his head hard.

"Bleed, you weakling!" his dad yelled at him, still laughing.

Then he came back to the cavern. He could feel the energy of Halo's shield around him. When he looked over at Kire, seeing double because his head was in so much pain, he noticed Kire's throwing him a thumbs-up. "Keep pushing forward! We can't let him escape!"

Kaos's bellowing scream of rage turned Trace to look his way. Kaos was on his knees, grabbing the sides of his face and clutching onto his crown. He was trying to delve into Rezin's mind.

"He's too strong!" Kaos shouted. "We need a new approach!"

Near him, Rose struggled to manipulate the plants around her. Her strength was fading. "He's right!" she called. "I-I don't know how much longer I can hold on!"

Trace tried to rally, forcing himself back to his feet. "We can't give up! Keep fighting!" Upon uttering the words, his swords flamed and suddenly burned a bit brighter. Still, Trace worried they were outmatched.

Then, in a sudden outburst, Rezin's wicked laughter echoed through the cavern. "Capture me?" he roared. "You think you can *contain* me?"

How did he figure it out?! Trace tried to find where Rezin's voice was coming from, but it was all around him. The teens exchanged confused glances. None of them knew how he figured it out.

What did this mean?

Fearing his retaliation, Trace ran with his sword toward Amberly, wanting to protect her from whatever Rezin's next move was. But then, wearing a twisted smile, Rezin appeared out of nowhere. He deliberately moved into the path of Trace and his fiery sword, impaling himself upon it before Trace even had a chance to think.

"NO!" Kaos shouted behind him as Trace stared at the bleeding, smiling alien, skewered by his sword. There was nothing to be done. Even when Trace, who had been brought down to the ground by the weight of Rezin slamming into him, quickly yanked his weapon out of the monster, the flames emitting from it engulfed him. And as Rezin lay there, burning alive, he bore a triumphant look in his eyes. "Yash's power... cannot be... contained."

Amberly reached out, her gauntlet summoning water from a nearby underground river to extinguish the flames. But it was too late. Rezin's body disintegrated into smoke and ash, leaving them all in unimaginable darkness.

What have I done?

Trace got to his feet, joining the others in stunned silence. In a single instant, their hopes had been shattered by Rezin's sacrifice. They had failed to capture him, and now his master, Yash, was going to destroy everything.

EPILOGUE

It didn't matter to Trace how many times he was told otherwise. He didn't believe anyone.

It was his fault that Rezin perished. He had only been thinking about getting to Amberly, about keeping her safe. She was all that mattered at that moment. He should have been paying better attention to his surroundings. Maybe then, he would have seen Rezin just in time to prevent him from moving in the way of his sword somehow.

Rezin, upon somehow realizing what he needed to do for his master, sacrificed his own life. Capturing Rezin had been the only chance The Unlikely Defenders had to prevent Yash, the great, evil, powerful entity, from descending upon the world in a storm of ruin.

Now, nothing could stop him. *They* couldn't stop him.

The realization of their failure hung heavy in the air around the quintets inside of that too-quiet cavern. They all knew what this meant. No one needed to utter a single word about it. Yash's impending destruction was now inevitable. Never before had their futures and the fate of the Earth realm been so uncertain.

When Amberly took Trace's hand in hers, Trace didn't pull away. But he couldn't meet her gaze either, despite how he could feel her eyes burning a hole in his cheek. He knew she only wanted to offer him words of comfort.

But Trace didn't want to hear them.

Instead, his gaze shifted toward Kaos, his friend-turned-rival. The strain that had settled between them seemed insoluble. His conversation with Amberly that they never got to finish still managed to clarify one thing. Kaos had conspired to push them toward breaking up. He had been the one to drive the wedge between Trace and Amberly. Looking back, remembering the way Kaos glued himself to Amberly's hip, how Trace watched him go out of his way to provide aid and comfort to Amberly when he'd never do that for anyone else, the way he tried to protect her as if she were his to save—it all made Trace feel so stupid for not realizing it sooner. Kaos was in love with Amberly.

And as Kaos stared at the hand of the girl he longed to win over, gripping tightly onto Trace's, Trace could see the darkness growing inside of him. A little bit of darkness grew inside Trace at that moment, too. They could have been stronger as a team if he hadn't crossed them. Now, Albus's words, his cryptic warning of the blackness festering within Kaos, clung on tightly to Trace's mind. How could any of them stop it? How could Trace get back together with Amberly and risk it only making Kaos sink further?

Their world was on the brink of ending, and they were the only five who knew about it. They were likely the only ones who could do anything about it. They had to clean up the mess they caused. In doing so, Trace knew that their unity and resilience would be tested like never before. From this moment on, his every action would be driven by his desperation to protect the things he held dear. To undo his wrongs. To fight for what was right.

Trace had no idea what the future held. But there was one thing in which he was certain: their gifts, their union, it was no longer enough to save the world. Not anymore.

AUTHOR'S NOTE

Dear Beloved Reader,

Thank you so much for continuing the journey with The Unlikely Defenders from Trace's point of view in The Unseemly Protectors.

I truly hope that you enjoyed it! If you did, I would be so grateful if you would consider leaving a review. Reviews help other readers find my work, so a review is very valuable to me.

The next book in the series will feature Kaos, and is called The Untimely Champions. Also, feel free to check out my other books!

https://swiy.co/UnlikelyDefenders

Visit my website at LilySkyy.com and interact with me on social media. Did you know that you could support me directly by purchasing books directly from my website instead of a third-party store? There's also awesome merch available for each of my series. Also, make sure to sign up for my mailing list to be the first to know about new releases and special happenings such as previews and give-a-ways!

I love getting feedback from my readers, and if you'd like to stay in touch (or discuss my books), join me over at the Lily Skyy Readers' Group. I'd also love to connect with you on Instagram, TikTok, and Twitter! Feel free to reach out to me directly via email at social@lilyskyy.com.

Again, I thank you for reading, and I can't wait to join you on the next adventure!

With heartfelt sincerity,

Lily Skyy